Grayson

THE BOUNTY KING BROTHERS
Novella 1

KAY MAREE

Contents:

Copyright © 2019 KAY MAREE...3
One...4
Two 11
Three 17
Four...26
Five 31
Six 39
Seven...44
Eight..49
Nine...56
Ten 73
Epilogue...88
About The Author..93
Author Links 94

GRAYSON

The Bounty King Brothers

Novella 1

Copyright © 2019 KAY MAREE.

Written by Kay Maree

Disclaimer

This story is a figment of the author's imagination.

All characters are fictional and are not intended to
represent anyone living or dead.

One

Grayson

"Johnson, what's up mate?" I push away from my desk and head towards the front of the office. I rest my forearm against the cool glass windows that line the front wall and look out towards the parking lot.

"Grayson, I just wanted to let you know Mac's on her way there now, she should be there any minute," I grunt in response as my attention is drawn to a pair of tanned legs. Letting my eyes travel up they take in a pair of tight black denim shorts moulded to the finest ass I have ever seen in my fucking life, bending at the waist under the hood of an old cherry red Cadillac. "Fucken shit," I mumble as I re-adjust my aching cock that's begging to be released from the confines of my black cargo pants.

"I gotta go mate, but thanks again for giving Mac this opportunity to work for you guys."

Snapping my attention back to the voice in my ear instead of the ass that's begging to be spanked I try to concentrate on what Mick is saying.

"No problem mate, mum's out today, so I will be the one to interview her."

"Fuck, don't fuck with my sister King," he grumbles. I chuckle at how well he knows me. We have known each other since we were kids and I didn't even know he had a sister till last week when he said his sister was coming to live with him. He told me she was in need of a job and didn't want to work at the Mechanic shop he runs. She was interested in becoming a Bounty Hunter one day, so she wanted an office job here to learn everything there is to know about what we do.

"Catch ya later mate," I end the call not making any promises as my attention is once again drawn to the fine piece of ass as the thump of the hood getting closed echoes around me. Stuffing my phone into my pants pocket I make my way out the front door wanting to get a better view. I'm not fucking disappointed either, it's like I'm fucking hypnotized as I watch waves of inky black hair with blonde highlights fall down her back as she turns the ignition off. Sounds of Prince's *Little Red Corvette* die on the wind. Turning towards me, her hair blows across her face, I grit my teeth together as her hips sway slightly making her way over towards me. Biting back a growl when she comes to a stop about a metre in front of me, not liking the distance between us. Sucking in a hard breath, my body tenses as her eyes take me in from head to toe, wanting her to like what she sees. My muscles tense when her bright honey coloured eyes lock with mine as a shy smile kisses what looks like natural red lips making my hard as fuck cock punch against the zipper of my pants. The air seems to thicken around us, background noises fade away and I'm left with my heartbeat echoing in my ears. We seem to be in a silent battle wondering who will speak first and I swallow a couple of times trying to get my voice working. Never in my life have I ever been speechless.

"Hi I'm Mac, I'm here for the interview with Mrs. Tanya King," she holds out her small hand and without even thinking I grip her soft hand with mine. I pull her a little closer as a gasp leaves her parted lips and the tip of her pink tongue swipes across her plump bottom lip. I fight everything in me to not slam my mouth down on hers wanting to know what she tastes like. Fuck. She looks nothing like the fucking photo Mick showed me last week when I agreed to this. If I had known this is what she really looked like I'm not sure if I would have fucking agreed to this. Fuck, who am I kidding? I would have moved the meeting up fucking sooner. Fuck she is a tiny little thing and sexy as fuck. She reminds me of one of them bomber girls that used to be painted on the side of the old fighter planes. Fuck I'm in trouble. After a moment I realise I still haven't said a damn word clearing my throat, her eyes snap back to mine as a ting of colour creeps into her cheeks at being caught checking me out. A hunger like no other before runs through me wanting her eyes on me and only me. Doing a quick sweep with my eyes around the parking lot I notice a few people around and I grit my teeth as a guy across the lot is blatantly staring straight at my girl. Fuck my girl where did that shit come from? Shaking my head, I need to get her inside before I go over and rip his eyes out of his fucking head.

"Name's Grayson and Tanya isn't here at the moment."

"Oh," her mouth forms a perfect O and I can't help picturing those lips wrapped around my cock. A growl slips free before I can stop it and I watch as her breathing picks up. A soft look washes over her doll-like face. Fuck she looks like she's been dipped in sex, but she has this shy-like quality to her that has my protective instincts kicking in and my already hard cock pulses with need. Clenching my jaw against the pain I'm trying to find my words when she speaks first.

"I can come back," she breathes out, innocence coating her words as her sweet scent seems to invade every one of my senses. How the fuck is this girl Mick's sister knowing Mick is an asshole and the only reason we have been mates for so long is because he gives us a good deal on the mechanics for our cars. I should step back and tell her to come back when mum is here but I just can't seem to get the words past my lips.

"It's fine, why don't we head in, and we can go over what the job entails," without giving her a chance to object I drop her hand. Turning slightly I place my hand on her lower back, feeling the shiver that races through her at my touch and I guide her towards the front door. Fuck what the hell is happening to me? A feeling like I have never felt before races through me. The ground seems to shake with each step I take and not only do I want to fuck this girl I can't help the feeling of her being mine and wanting to mark every single inch of silky-smooth skin on her body. Holy fucking shit I want to claim this girl and lock her away from the rest of the world no matter how irrational that thought is.

***

Guiding her towards the chair in front of my desk I wait for her to take her seat before going around the other side and taking mine. I grunt not liking the distance between us but know I also need a little space between us, so I can get my head on straight. Taking a deep breath, I rummage through the paperwork scattered across the black glossy surface of my desk till I locate the manila folder mum placed there yesterday. Finally finding it I flip it open and scan the information her brother gave to us.

Mackenzie Stevens. Fuck her name even drips sex and I can't help the bite of disappointment when I realise I'm 8 years older than her. Worry swims through me at the thought she probably wouldn't be interested in a 30-year-old man. Fuck it, I'll show her that I'm the only man on her radar and no other males will ever have a chance with her.

"Mr. King," she murmurs. Snapping my eyes to hers I watch as she fidgets with her fingers in her lap.

"Mr. King is my father," I grunt. "Do you always wear this for interviews?" I make a show of taking in every stitch of clothing moulded to every perfect curve of her luscious as fuck body right down to the black converse covering her feet.

"I.. Um..." she shakes her head, clenching her hands into fists on her lap. "No, I just got into town when Mick called me and told me about the interview and I didn't have time to go back to his place and change." Her fingers unclench and she tries to tug the ends of her shorts down her smooth thighs. I grit my teeth at the motion wanting nothing more than to reach over and drag the shorts higher up. Nodding my head, I go back to the folder in my hands. I look to her last employer and see she worked for Chance Bounty's in Surfers Paradise Queensland.

"Why did you leave Chance Bounty's," I ask noticing how gruff my voice has become. Chance Bounty's, as far as I know, is pretty well run.

"I needed a change," she says simply looking anywhere but at me. There's something more there and I wonder if I push, she will tell me.

"Is that all?"

"Um, can we call it a difference of opinions, for now, please," a slight begging tone laces her words and I can't help imagine what she would look like on her knees begging for my cock.

"For now," I manage to get out as I try to think of anything other than the image I just put into my head. She seems to relax at my words and lays her hands flat on her thighs. Sliding all the tax and employment forms across to her she leans forward and grabs the pen I hand her and begins to fill them out. My eyes are drawn to the dip at the front of her black halter top with white polka dots as the hint of her cleavage peeks out. My hands clench the folder still in my hands knowing they would fit perfectly. Locking my jaw, I try to breathe through my nose and I'm not sure if that's worse as the smell of coconut with a hint of lime invades my nose.

Fucken shit, what is it about this girl that has my head spinning? My knee begins to bounce on its own accord and my control is splintering by the second. Her curves, the shy smile, her scent all that combined has my world spinning, never in my life has this ever happened to me.

"First thing tomorrow morning I need you to be here, and we can run through what you will be doing." Fuck I'm amazed I could get so many words out. Blowing out a hard breath I know I need to put some distance between us, so I can get my head on straight. How the fuck am I supposed to work with this chick when all I can think about is bending her over my desk and taking what I've wanted since the first moment I saw her. Fuck what would it be like to see my handprint on her ass as she begs for me to fill her greedy pussy with my cock and sucking up every bit of cum I have to give her. My cock punches against my zipper wanting exactly that. I need to mark her, claim her so no other asshole thinks they can take her away from me. Fuck I need to breed her with my baby, having her round with my baby would definitely say she is off fucking limits.

"So, I have the job," her excited voice penetrates my fucked-up head and all I can do is nod not trusting my voice. Not believing my thought process right now but I can't help replaying what my father always told me and my brothers.

"When you meet the other half of your soul, the ground will seem to fall out underneath you and nothing else in the world will matter except her." I always thought he was full of shit and just because that's what happened when he met our mother doesn't mean it would happen for us. That instant love shit I always thought was total bullshit, but right now in this moment, the bottom of my world just dropped out underneath me and shifted. Everything else has fallen away and the only thing that matters right now is Mackenzie. I feel like I have been rolled over by a steamroller and I can only hope she is feeling everything that I am. If not I'm a ruthless motherfucker and I always get what I want, I'm also a patient man which is why I'm fucking excellent at my job and one way or another I know this woman will be mine.

Two

Mackenzie

I don't know what the hell is going on right now. My body is going crazy like I have just been electrocuted, my stomach is filled with butterflies and I have to keep sucking my tongue to get words out. The minute I turned around after locking my car everything inside me started firing on all pistons. When I started to move towards him my legs were shaky and threatened to give out with each step closer. Closer to the mountain of a man with tattooed arms crossed tight across a massive chest. I tried to act confident but I think I completely stuffed it up and came off as a shy awkward teenager again not knowing what to do or say. Once I was a metre away I tried to ignore the beating of my heart that echoed through my ears and I took in his size. I barely came up to his shoulders and then when he turned his sharp piercing green eyes on me, I felt at any second, I was going to be a pool of hot burning need at his feet. Just the way his muscles flexed in his arm as he ran his hand through his messy midnight black hair nearly had me panting. Before I lost complete control, I remembered what my step-brother said on the phone about the group of brothers that work here being a bunch of players. I was worried until he told me they were the best in the business and could teach me a lot, so they can be players all they want. I'm just here to learn and to make a living.

Looking at this guy now as he sits across the black glossy desk covered in paperwork from me, I worry I may be in over my head. Could I actually handle seeing him every day let alone all over random women? A bit of jealousy spikes through me not liking the thought and I don't have any right feeling this way. He isn't mine and I sure as shit ain't his. I just need to get through this interview and then hopefully I would barely have to see him. From what Mick says The Bounty King's needed another office lady because up till this point Tanya their mother is doing it all by herself as her boys are usually out chasing the bail jumpers. I'm glad he didn't push for more about why I left Queensland cause I'm not too sure what more to tell him. I do not know if him and the owner of Chance's Bounty, Paul, are friends and I didn't want to lessen my chances of getting this job cause this is what I want to do. I know my step-brother said I can work for him but we barely get along at the best of times. The only reason I'm staying with him is that his father insisted I stay there. Even though he is no longer married to my mother he still cares about me and what I do. God knows my mother never gave a shit, all she ever cared about was her next fix and how she could get it. Shivers race through me as his deep husky voice washes over me snapping me out of my head.

"First thing tomorrow morning I need you to be here, and we can run through what you will be doing," his voice is so gruff that it seems to ignite something deep inside me. Something I have never felt before and right now I can't afford to have this feeling, especially for someone that is known to sleep with every woman he meets. I won't be another notch on anyone's bedpost.

"So, I have the job?" I ask excited and a little disappointed that I have to wait till tomorrow but maybe it's for the best. It might be enough time to get my body's reaction to this man to cool its friggin jets.

"Thank you," I push to my feet getting ready to leave, needing out of this office. The heat outside is nothing compared to the temperature inside this space.

"I'll walk you out."

All I do is nod not trusting my voice right now as he makes his way back around the desk and rests his hand at the base of my spine. The heat from his palm radiates through me like molten lava running through my veins, making heat creep into my cheeks. Trying to shake off the feeling I make my way towards the door when it flies open and three huge bodies take up the open space.

"Well, hello there beautiful," Oh damn he's smooth I think, swiping my tongue across my lip before sucking it into my mouth as a sexy smirk curls his lip and a dimple pops out. I can't help wondering if Grayson has a dimple under that thick five o'clock shadow, he's sporting. They all look so similar and my mouth dries knowing full well why girls throw themselves at these boys. Built, full of tattoos, black cargo pants paired with either black Henley singlets or a black wife beater, strapped up in bulletproof vests with their gold badges hanging around their necks.

"Shut the fuck up and cut the shit Tanner," Grayson growls from behind me. I feel the vibration from his chest run down my spine only now realising how close he really is to me. As he says the words he snakes a strong arm around my waist, pulling me back into his hard chest and I try not to melt into his hold. The slow caress of the tips of his fingers against my belly through my shirt has goosebumps racing across my skin and I can't help relaxing into his hold. Well shit damn, this is not helping my head to keep distance from him, but holy shit, I have never been so turned on in all my life.

"I… Ah… better go," I rush out as the three men in front of me seem to study their brother who still has his arm around me before cracking up laughing. Before I can move, the one that called me beautiful puts his hand out to shake mine and the other two follow suit.

"I'm Tanner, that's Phoenix and Maverick," he points to the men behind him, and they nod saying hi as a smirk kisses their lips.

"Hi, I'm Mac," I shake each of their hands.

"Move," Grayson grunts out from behind me and I freeze in his arms at how clipped his voice is. I go to take a step away but he just holds me firm, looking up over my shoulder I notice he is staring at his brothers, as a tic starts in his jaw. Turning back to the brothers I bite my lip to stop the laugh that wants to spill free as each one winks at me before walking past us. I can't hold it in anymore when Grayson grunts as if he just got elbowed in the gut.

"He is so fucked," I hear one mumble low as the rest agree and I'm not sure who the hell said it but I'm confused as to what they mean by it.

"Let me walk you to your car," his hot breath skates down my neck and has that molten lava feeling racing straight between my legs as what started out as a slow ache has now turned straight into a throbbing need. I feel the arm around me relax and before he can stop me, I head out the front door heading straight to my car. I need to be outside and not wrapped in his arms with his intoxicating scent surrounding me. It's making my head spin with the possibility of letting this man touch me right where I ache. Before I can open my door, I'm swung around and pushed up against the door. Before I can say anything Grayson steps into my space, so close my breasts brushes against his hard chest. I suck in a deep breath when the cool metal from his badge seeps through my shirt making my nipples harden.

"Shit," I gasp.

"Tell me I'm not the only one," he rasps out, tucking a wayward strand of hair behind my ear before the tips of his fingers slide down the side of my cheek. Looking into his smokey green eyes that seem darker now that I'm so close, my mind blanks and I can't remember what he just asked me.

"Mackenzie," the way he breathes out my name makes him sound like he is in pain. Shifting my legs a little I try to squeeze my thighs together to dull the ache. Before I can get the chance he pushes his leg between mine adding a little pressure, and as much as I fight it a small moan slips free from my throat.

"Fuck you do don't you," he grunts pushing against me again. Everything else around us disappears as the pressure increases. Before I know what's happening, I'm gripping his shoulders. He hisses out against my neck at the bite of pain from my nails and I know I really should push him away but another a part of me wants everything he has to give me. My eyes roll back in my head as my body comes alive at the touch of his tongue on my neck but before I can scream out, he swoops down and takes my lips in a bruising kiss, sucking each of my whimpers down. My body goes lax against the car as my head comes down from the most amazing high I have ever felt. A low rumble vibrates against my chest as the word "Mine," hits my ears and my head chooses that moment to snap back to the present. Shit, what did I just do? Pushing against his chest he backs up a step and it's enough room for me to open the car door and quickly slip into the driver's seat.

"See you tomorrow princess," he smirks running his tongue across his bottom lip as if needing more of my taste. Shit, I can't let this man get to me. I need him to know I will not become one of his many women.

"Mr. King, trust me that is the last taste you will get of me. I won't be another notch in your bedpost," I push as much confidence in my words that I can muster and before he can say anything else, I start the engine. Music blasts away whatever reply he had to say. Putting my cherry baby into gear I quickly reverse before heading out the parking lot driveway. All the while I watch in my rearview mirror at Grayson standing there with his arms crossed over his chest and a serious look on his face. I can't help the little thrill that shoots through me at the feeling this game he's playing has only just begun.

Three

Grayson

I watch as Mackenzie turns out of the parking lot kicking myself for how fast I moved with her. I had planned to take my time but the way my brothers were looking at her pissed me off. I needed to stake my fucking claim before they got it in their heads that they even had a chance. Possessiveness like nothing I have ever felt before slammed into me and I needed to know she felt the same. I felt the way her body melted into mine and it took everything in me not to throw her over my shoulder and take her home with me. Shaking my head at myself I need to pull my ass in line and work out a way to make her believe she won't be just another notch in my bedpost. No fucking way will that happen, she will be the one and fucking only from this moment on.

Now I just need to work out how I'm going to convince her.

"Fuck," I grumble raking my hand through my hair as I make my way back inside wanting to kick my brother's asses and make sure they know to stay the fuck away from my girl. Fuck it's been years since I have had a girlfriend. I work too damn much and my last girlfriend decided spreading her fucking legs for some other fuckwit was a better option. But I have never felt this need to claim anyone before and I know Mackenzie is the one. Without her saying a fucking word I know that she felt the exact same thing.

Pushing through the glass doors I stop in my tracks, folding my arms across my chest as three shit eating grins stare straight at me.

"That's one fine piece of ass brother," Tanner comments nodding his head towards the glass windows. A low growl rumbles in my chest when he calls her just a piece of ass. Seeming to like my reaction he throws his head back on a deep laugh.

"A piece of ass that seemed to race out of here like the hounds of hell were chasing her down," Phoenix chuckles spiking my anger more I'm walking a fine line right now and I'm about to fucking snap just as Maverick opens his big fucking mouth.

"She must have a sweet pussy to have you looking like you're ready to kill." Before he can utter another word I have him pinned by the throat to the wall, photos shake from the impact. But right now, I'm not thinking clearly.

"Shit brother," Maverick gasps reaching up and grabbing my wrists trying to pull me off him while Tanner and Phoenix try to pull me back.

"Fuck, brother, we were only fucking with you," Tanner grunts out.

"What," I grit out.

"Grayson we ain't fucking stupid you had the same look on your face that dad gets when he looks at mum," Phoenix grumbles.

Loosening my hold around Maverick's throat a little I take a few deep breaths trying to calm my ass down.

"What the fuck," I grunt.

"Mum told us about Mac coming in today, and we wanted to see how fucking serious you were, considering we have to work with her if you fuck this shit up," Tanner shrugs his shoulders. Obviously he thinks what he is saying makes perfect fucking sense as the other two dipshits nod their heads like a bunch of bobble-head dolls.

"She's mine," I growl out. "She ain't just a piece of ass or some fucking pussy so watch your fucking mouths," I grunt letting Maverick go as the pricks start laughing their asses off.

"Then why the fuck did she race out of here like someone was chasing her?" Maverick grunts rubbing his throat. Running both my hands through my hair I pull on the ends a little remembering what she said before she peeled out of here.

"She doesn't want to be another notch in my bedpost," I grunt repeating her words getting pissed she would even think that.

"Who the fuck said she would be?" Tanner asks

"Fuck knows," I answer. "She said she just got into town and that's why she wasn't dressed more appropriate for the interview so it's not like she had time for someone to talk shit to her about me," I mumble.

"She was dressed just fine to me," Phoenix quips and I reach over and punch him in the arm making him grunt. "Watch it brother," I growl, he smirks but wisely closes his fucking mouth. This is nothing new with us we always give each other shit and me being the eldest I'm usually the worst one. Right now, I don't have time to fuck around. I need to work out how to get her to believe this isn't just a one-time deal, this is a life fucking sentence.

"How did she know about the interview if she just got into town today?" Tanner asks to no-one in particular and it slams into me why she would say that.

"Fucking Mick," I growl in frustration.

"Mick Johnson?" Maverick asks

Nodding I reply. "Yeah it's her fucking brother. Fuck I should have put two and two together. He warned me on the phone not to fuck with his sister. He must have planted some shit in her head that I'm some kind of fucking player or some shit," anger wells in the pit of my stomach, nothing could be further from the truth.

"Well big brother looks like you have your work cut out for you," Phoenix says patting me on the back chuckling.

"Fuck," I blow out a hard breath.

"Look let's deal with this shit later right now we have a case so let's track this fucker down before we lose our 20k."

Following my brothers towards the back I know I need to get my head in the game and work this shit out with Mackenzie later. I cannot afford to have my head elsewhere while we hunt.

"Name is James Parsons aka The Ringmaster," Tanner says as he starts writing on the whiteboard attached to the back wall. Maverick starts up his computer so James' arrest record flicks up on the 60-inch flat screen that's mounted on the wall next to the whiteboard. My father has this old-school way about him when it comes to the whiteboard but with so much technology around these days my brother's and I prefer to use the flat screen. But God forbid we got rid of the whiteboard. My father may be semi-retired now but that doesn't mean we would disrespect his ways and the ways we were taught. Phoenix and I lean against our desks that line both side walls.

"Current Charges?" I ask looking at the Wanted A4 poster sized displayed on the screen.

"Assault - Reckless Grievous Bodily harm on his ex-girlfriend. He missed his court date yesterday so we need to find him now," Tanner grits out pissed so I'm guessing this was his bond. "He's looking at 10 to 14 years in a cell so he fucking ran."

"Fuck, scum of the earth hitting a fucking woman," I grit out feeling adrenaline spike through me wanting to get this piece of shit. My brothers all murmur their agreement, we were brought up to treat women with respect and to never raise a hand to them. It grates my fucking nerves hearing this shit. My father may be big and scary as fuck but when it comes to my mother, she is the motherfucking boss and no-one messes with her. If she doesn't get you my father sure as hell will. "Who co-signed his bail?" Maverick asks swiping his fingers over the keyboard of his computer.

"His roommate, Nathan Wills," Tanner reads off the file in his hands.

"Do we know why they call him The Ringmaster?" Maverick asks running his fingers through his beard he always does that when he's thinking.

"Apparently he runs his own crew. Drugs, weapons, prostitutes anything he can get his hands on," Tanner shrugs.

I study the picture again taking in every little detail not wanting to miss a thing. The picture makes him look like he's coked off his brains with wild dark eyes. He has a scar across his eyebrow and he looks like he stuck his finger in a power point as blonde hair sticks out everywhere.

"So, he's a badass motherfucker," Phoenix chuckles.

"Yeah but we're fucking meaner brother," Maverick laughs bumping knuckles with Phoenix.

"Phoenix, call Nathan and see if we can get a lead on James' whereabouts."

Nodding, Phoenix rounds his desk and starts to dial the number. Phoenix is one of the best to get information out of anyone. He could talk shit till the cows come home and there is something about him that has people spilling their guts.

"Hello," comes over the speakerphone.

"James?"

"Nah mate, this is Nathan."

"I need James man, where's he at?" Phoenix sounds like he is jonesing for a hit.

"Who dis?"

"Jimmy, we used to kick it, we go way back but I've been in the joint and just got out. I'm jonesing man," Phoenix makes a pained noise.

"He not here, he down at the park. What you need?"

"Fuck man, I need a gram which park he at?"

"Down by the foreshore."

"Thanks, man," Phoenix groans out before clicking off.

"Fuck I swear you love fucking with people's heads," Tanner chuckles making a shit-eating grin spread across Phoenix's face.

"Alright let's get this shit done," I grunt needing to fill my head with something other than the taste of my girl on my tongue. Pushing away from my desk I head towards the wooden cupboard against the far wall that holds our shit.

"Let's get strapped up," I say grabbing my belt with my mace, handcuffs attached. Grabbing my radio, I clip it to the top of my bulletproof vest. We are all licensed to carry guns but we keep them locked in the safe. We choose not to use them as we would rather bring the jumpers in without serious injury plus the four of us ain't small by any means. We keep in shape and know how to bring a guy down.

"Boys," my mother's sweet voice fills the room and I turn around and see my father studying the board as mum walks over and hugs us all in turn. My mum is as sweet as pie but tough as fucking nails. Nothing gets past her and she proves me right when she makes it to me and pulls me into a hug before pulling back with a huge smile on her face. Even at the age of 55 she is still beautiful with long brown hair scattered with a few strands of gray, the only sign showing her actual age with kind, sharp, brown eyes. She is a tiny thing, barely making it to our shoulders whereas we get our height from our dad. Tanner and I got his black hair and green eyes but Phoenix and Maverick got mums brown hair and brown eyes.

"What," I ask smiling. Her smile is infectious and you can't help but return it no matter what mood you're in.

"I heard you found your girl today," she places her warm palm against my cheek. She has done that since we were kids and it never fails her from getting what she wants. Looking over her head I eyeball my brothers as they try to cover up their smirks. Dumb asses the lot of them. Fuck, wait till they are in my position, bloody mummy boys the lot of them.

"Mackenzie," I answer bringing my attention back to my mother.

"Isn't that the girl that came in for the interview today," she smirks already knowing the answer.

"Yep," I nod clenching my teeth as dad chuckles and pats me on the back.

"Your world fell apart out from under you didn't it?" he smiles waiting for me to tell him he's right and as much as it sucks to admit it, I find myself smiling.

"Sure fucking did dad," I chuckle making him laugh harder.

"Bout fucking time," he says as he makes his way towards the front office.

"Grayson, you treat this girl right, you'd better have given her the job. I'm getting too old for all this stuff on my own," her face and tone of voice is stern now and I know not to fuck with her.

"Yep I sure did and I plan on it mum, she's it for me." I kiss her cheek before she walks away towards the office my father went into.

"Fucking pack of bitches the lot of you, can't keep your fucking big mouths shut for five minutes before you're ringing your mummy and gossiping like old women."

"Us? what about you?" they laugh. "You could have told her no," Maverick says.

"Fuck no and get caught lying, fuck that I would rather go head on with a hundred of these pricks than face her wrath," I point to the flat screen at the wanted image. We break out into laughter before they agree completely. You don't lie to our mother unless you are prepared to take the hiding she would give you if she found out and in this family nothing stays a fucking secret for long.

Four

Mackenzie

Sleep last night was bloody hopeless. Eventually, I gave up and pulled my Kindle out. I started *Heal Me Book 3 in the Reapers Reign MC series by Aleisha Maree.* I preordered it a while ago, and I was so excited when I saw it pop up in my files. I'm not sure how long I was reading for. All I remember is waking up to my alarm going off with my Kindle on my face and my bedside lamp still on. Groaning I roll over and bury my head into my pillow needing another few minutes. Pushing up on my knees I groan stretching, damn I feel it in every muscle that I didn't sleep well last night. My traitorous body comes alive with the realisation of seeing Grayson again today and I'm pissed at myself 'cause nothing good could ever come from allowing that man to touch me.

"Shit damn," I grunt pushing off the bed and making my way towards the small en suite in my new room. My space isn't much to look at but it's enough for me. It's not like I had a lot to move anyways, everything I need fitted into my car. My car, the only thing I have that's worth anything to me and it's not because it's worth a fair bit. No, it's because when I was a little girl, I used to help my father fix it up and when he died it became mine. I knew the minute my mum tried to sell it that it was time to leave and get the hell away from her. Turning the taps on I sniff back the tears that threaten to fall, lifting my face towards the spray of the hot water I try to relax and soak in the heat.

"Hey Mac, do you want breakfast?"

My silent blissful moment is broken by Mick's sleazy voice and I let out a scream when I realise he's walked straight into the bathroom. Quickly wrapping the shower curtain around me I peek my head out just in time to see him looking me up and down, disgust runs up and down my spine as bile rises up my throat. Sucking it back down I try to get words out.

"Get out," I shout.

Chuckling at my reaction it grates down my spine as he blatantly checks me out.

"Now no need to be like that, I called out but you didn't hear me the first time," he grunts rubbing his chin as his eyes squint at me. Oh, my god, as if that's a fucking excuse to waltz in here while I'm naked. This is why I was skeptical about living here with him cause the last time I was here he got drunk and thought it was a good idea to try to hit on me. The gross thing about it is he tells people I'm his sister when in truth, I'm just his step-sister. He thinks because we are not blood-related that we would eventually get together.

"Can you get out please? I have to get ready for work," I murmur as a chill seeps into my bones not too sure how he would act. I could put up a good fight against him, he's about my height but twice my size with a pot-belly, always in a filthy white wife beater and greased up work pants. The minute I turned up here yesterday I should have gotten back in my car and left to find a hotel room but my stepdad said the last time Mick hit on me he was drunk and didn't know what he was doing. But with him right here, right now in the bathroom, I know it was no mistake. He meant everything then, and he thinks with me under his roof this time shit will be different.

"Remember what I said about the King brother's Mac and when you get home from work, we will grab dinner or something," he spits out before walking out of the bathroom. He doesn't bother to close the door. Shit, I don't know what kind of mind tricks he is trying to play with me but I'm not fucking interested and there is no way I'm hanging around to find out. I need to get my shit together and get the hell out of here. After work I'll find a hotel to stay at till I can work out where I can go. Luckily I didn't completely unpack my car I think as I reach forward and grab a towel off the railing on the wall. I try to not let the curtain slip through my fingers. God only fucking knows if dipshit is still around wanting to have a look.

***

Pulling into a spare car park out the front of the Bounty King's I take it all in. Now that a mountain of a man isn't taking up my full focus. Roof to ground windows lines the front of the office with the Bounty King's logo plastered on the front all in gold with a crown at the top. Five stars lay underneath with the words "Bounty Kings" in fancy script underneath the stars. It's quite stylish and I wonder if Tanya designed it. Making my way towards the front doors, I stop short a couple of steps away when it flies open. Phoenix steps out and smiles when his dark brown eyes meet mine.

"Morning gorgeous," he drawls out as smooth as silk and if I was anybody else and didn't spend the bloody night thinking of his brother my panties may have combusted on the spot. Shit, did I really just admit to myself that I couldn't get his brother off my mind. Shit, shit, shit, shaking my head I push the thought away for another time as the heat begins to creep up my neck. "How are you this bright sunny day?" he smiles snapping me back to the present and god damn it, I know I can't hide the heat creeping into my cheeks this time. His smile hits me full force and it's so infectious I can't stop my mouth from curling up matching his. Just like that the shit from this morning slowly starts to fade away.

"Good thank you," I manage to get out before a deep growl pulls my attention towards the front door where Grayson is standing looking pissed off.

"Go get the fucking coffee Nix before I beat your ass," he grunts curling his fingers into a fist at his side.

"Sure thing big brother," he chuckles "You wanna come with me Mackenzie?" he winks, my name coming out as smooth as silk again he reaches out to take my hand. Before I can register what the hell is happening, I'm pushed behind a hard broad back, and my eyes take in how tense his muscles are as they strain against his tight black Henley vest. Before I even realise what I'm doing I rest my hands against his waist and immediately feel some of the tension leave his body.

"Fuck off Nix before I punch you in the face and from now on you call her Mac," he grunts and I don't understand why he doesn't want him to call me by my full name.

"Catch you later sexy," Phoenix calls out looking around Grayson before quickly jumping back laughing his ass off. He misses the punch Grayson throws out and I can't help but laugh with him.

"Fucking shit stirring little prick," Grayson grunts out turning to face me so now my hands rest against his hard stomach and my fingers twitch wishing it was bare skin I was touching. Shaking myself of those thoughts I go to take a step back but Grayson grabs my hands before I can move putting his arms around my waist pulling me in tight. His intoxicating scent assaults my nose making my head spin. Bending forward he plants a soft kiss to my forehead and something about the simple move softens my resolve to stay away from this man a little more.

"I missed you," he breathes out at the top of my head. "Fuck you smell good," I freeze in his strong arms wondering what the hell is happening right now.

"Um…What?" I breathe out looking up into his smokey green eyes that seem to lock with mine refusing to let me pull away.

"Come on Princess, let me introduce you to mum and dad." The way he says that makes me think it's more than just meeting my new employer's. Nodding my head not trusting my voice I let him lead the way. When he releases me I think he is about to walk back inside but instead he reaches down and locks his fingers with mine. The heat from his palm has all those feelings from yesterday rushing back through my veins and I'm not sure how much longer I can fight to keep my distance or even if I really want to. There is something about this man that makes me feel like this is what I have been missing my whole life but I'm so friggin scared of being hurt or this not meaning anything besides another conquest for him.

Five

Grayson

Having Mackenzie back in my space again settles the need I've had since she peeled out of here yesterday. I have been worrying all morning that she wouldn't turn up today and I was getting ready to go beat down Mick's door to find her. All this shit about taking it slow with her went out the fucking window the minute I kissed her. I'm hungry for another taste, but first I need to introduce her to mum and dad. After the introductions are done, I'm going to make sure she knows that she is mine from this day forward and I won't stop till she's in my bed screaming my name, every night for the rest of her god damn life. She can deny it all she wants but I know it's a lie and whatever fucked up shit her brother has been filling her pretty little head with needs to be sorted the fuck out and fast. She is mine and I'm done fucking waiting, I didn't sleep for shit last night wanting her with me.

"Oh, look at you," my mum comes out of the shared office with her hands out ready to hug my girl. Without letting her go I take a step to the side so she has enough room to give her a hug, my mum gives me the stink eye but I focus on my father when he comes out of the office and he starts laughing.

"Grayson," my mum snaps bringing my attention back to her and the sweet smile she had before is long gone.

"What," I grunt trying not to let that look get to me.

"Let her go," she pouts slamming her hands on her hips. Fuck I haven't touched my girl since yesterday but I know my mum won't let up. I feel the bite of Mackenzie's nails in the back of my hand and I look over and see a puzzled look on her face and before she can say anything I swoop down and place my lips on hers for a soft quick kiss. Making her gasp I fight the urge not to slip my tongue into her mouth and taste her sweetness.

"Fine," I grumble letting her go, folding my arms across my chest.

"Don't you have work to do?" mum grumbles as a smirk kisses her lips. She is trying to stir me and from my father's chuckle, he knows it too. But in all honesty I do have a lot of shit to do 'cause that fuck from last night slipped through our fingers and we need to chase him the fuck down. My mind has been complete shit all morning waiting for my woman to get here. I just grunt in response as dad makes his way over toward us.

"I hope I'm dressed okay?" Mackenzie mumbles in my mother's ear and it's only now I take in what she's wearing. Tight black jeans that look moulded to her ass, red Doc Martens and another one of those halter tops, but this one is red with black polka dots on it. Her midnight hair is up in a ponytail, the ends brushing the middle of her back. They are just begging to be wrapped around my fist and pulled back while I take her hard from behind, or riding me as her nails scrape down my chest marking me as hers. Her head thrown back in pure ecstasy. I bite back a groan at the images flashing through my head as my semi-hard cock turns to a full blown hard on. I'm just glad my parents are paying attention to my girl and not me right now as I adjust myself.

"You are dressed just fine lovely," my mother says resting her palm against her cheek. Mackenzie blinks a few times as if she is trying not to cry and I see my mum notices also.

"Okay so let's get started, this is my husband Derrek and if any of my boys pisses you off and I'm not around you tell him and he will sort them out okay?"

Chuckling Mackenzie nods her head "Okay," she murmurs.

"Okay, so the boys are on a case at the moment. I will bring you up to speed and show you where your desk is. I just sent Phoenix out to grab some food for all of us, so while we wait, we may as well jump in and get started."

"Sounds great," Mackenzie replies and goes to follow mum and dad but I snag her hand bringing her back into my chest. Bringing my thumb up I wipe a tear away that was caught in her thick eyelashes.

"Are you okay baby?" I whisper.

"Yeah I'm fine," she smiles. I can tell it's a little forced but I don't want to push her right now. So instead, I bend down and take her lips in a soft kiss, sliding my tongue across her bottom lip I steal a little taste. I hope to God it's enough to hold me over till later. Reaching down I give her ass a small squeeze causing her to whimper into my mouth and making me growl. Pulling back, I watch as a sweet smile curves her lips as heat begins to creep into her cheeks, I can't help running my fingers lightly over the heated flesh.

"I should stay away from you," she whispers.

"You're never getting rid of me now babe so stop fighting it," I growl watching her eyes widen. Her breathing picks up speed but before she can respond I take her lips in another kiss groaning as the taste of cherries explodes across my tongue from her lip gloss. Pulling back, I turn her towards my mum's office and smack her on the ass.

"Go before I take your ass right here for every motherfucker to see," I say between clenched teeth. Looking over her shoulder she winks as a sexy smirk kisses her lips.

"Tease," I growl making her laugh as she heads towards my mum.

***

I'm about at my wits end right now. If Phoenix doesn't stop flirting with my girl, I'm going to kick his ass. He knows exactly what he's doing too because every time he makes her blush, and she ducks her head he smirks over at me.

"Stop letting him get to you brother," Tanner chuckles.

"Easy for you to fucking say," I grunt at his ass as I push away from my desk.

"Phoenix get the fuck away from her. Now!" I clip the last word out hard so he gets that I'm pissed.

"Grayson" Mackenzie snaps "you're being rude."

Fuck a few hours with my mother, and she has the serious tone down. Not wanting to piss her off I hold back my anger and face my brother who has a shit-eating grin on his face.

Cock-sucker doesn't learn. "Fuck. Off. Please," I hiss out the please making him laugh his ass off, but he wisely moves away. Moving around her desk that I placed only a few feet away from mine needing her close,

I reach out my hand and wait for her to take it. After a few seconds she places her small palm in mine and I pull her to her feet and make my way out the back door needing to be alone with her. Once we are outside, I let go of her hand and begin to pace trying to calm my ass down as she leans against the building.

"I'm sorry," she murmurs halting me in my tracks before she can blink, I slam both hands either side of her head caging her in, her breathing picks up as her honey eyes meet mine.

"What are you sorry for?" I whisper a breath away from her lips trying to control myself.

"For snapping at you," she whispers.

"Babe I'm not pissed at you, I like that you're not afraid to snap at me, in fact it turns me the fuck on." I push the lower half of my body against hers, catching the hitch in her breath when she feels how hard I am. Planting a small kiss to her nose I breathe out who I'm pissed at "I'm pissed at my brother."

"Why?" she questions

"Because you're fucking mine and he needs to back the fuck off," I grunt.

"I'm not anybody's," strength laces her words as she straightens her shoulders.

"Like fuck, you have been mine since you drove into this parking lot."

"I will not be just another conquest for you. I'm not interested in a one-night stand," she shoves against my chest to try and get me to move. She's strong but I'm fucking stronger and I need her to know that's not what this is once and for all.

"You are the motherfucking prize babe, the only fucking notch on my bedpost that I'll ever fucking want or need. I know we just met but fuck don't you get it, you're it for me, you're my other half." I force the words out between clenched teeth needing her to get exactly what I fucking mean saying these words to her. Staring into my eyes I hope she sees the truth to my words.

"I'd better be the only one," she whispers with a hard edge after another moment and my already hard cock pushes against my zipper loving the possessiveness in her tone.

"You'd better fucking believe it and same goes for you too," I growl cupping her pussy between her legs, the heat of her pussy sends my pulse racing as a gasp leaves her mouth. I try to ignore my hard cock that's begging to be released. Bending down I take her lips in a hard kiss as I move my palm in a circular motion over her hard clit sucking down her little moans. Her body tenses but before I let her fall over the edge on a hard and fast orgasm I pull my lips from hers and a small whine escapes her throat.

"This is mine," I grunt making a slow motion with my palm again, causing her to shiver in my arms as her deep warm breaths wash over my face as the hint of lime fills my nostrils making me growl.

"Mackenzie, say it," I demand trying to control the fire coursing through me just from that little taste.

"It's yours," she pants trying to move her hips but I bring my other hand down and pin her to the brick wall.

"What else is mine?" I ask needing her to say it.

"Me," she whimpers as I start moving my palm a little bit faster now.

"That's right and don't you forget it."

"That makes you mine also, I couldn't share you," she breathes out as her forehead falls against my chest. Bending I nip the lobe of her ear then suck it into my mouth to soothe the sting before whispering in her ear.

"Never Princess, I'm yours and only yours," turning her face to mine I take her lips in a deep kiss, groaning when her tongue swipes along mine. I moan into her mouth as her body gives way to the orgasm I was holding her back from. Pulling back from the kiss I rest my forehead against hers while I let her catch her breath.

"Sexiest thing I have ever seen babe, and tonight I'm gonna make you scream my name," I promise as a fire ignites in her eyes and under the sun's rays they seem to glow.

"Promise?" she looks up at me through her thick lashes and my hard cock strains against my zipper.

"Princess, I'm going to make you burn for me so by the time I get you home tonight you will be begging for my cock to fill that pretty pussy." The breaths are coming heavier now and all I want to do is fuck her right here but her moans of pleasure are for my ears only. Turning her in my hold before I say fuck it, I smack her ass before pushing her towards the back door watching as she sways that fucking ass. Before pushing through the door, she gives me a sexy smile over her shoulder.

"I'm already there, Player," she winks pushing open the door making me growl, quickly taking up the space between us I smack her ass again, chuckling when a small whimper slips past her lips. "Don't tease me Princess," I murmur in her ear before heading to my desk. "Fuck," I grumble suppressing a groan as I take a seat, I'm as hard as fucking stone. Maverick laughs out loud from beside me probably at the pained expression on my fucking face.

"Asshole," I grunt turning towards my computer making him laugh harder.

Six

Mackenzie

Sitting back at my desk I try re-arranging all the files scattered across the black glossy surface. Trying to think of anything else besides what just happened out back. Holy fucken shit I'm so keyed up right now. I think if he even breathes in my direction right now, I would probably jump him. My cheeks heat, tingles dance down my spine as my thoughts race thinking that's the second time he has given me an orgasm in the past forty-eight hours and hasn't asked for anything in return. I bite my lip remembering his sweet delicious promise for tonight. I'm so consumed in my thoughts that I jump a little at the sound of Grayson's deep voice booming across the room.

"Mick what are you doing down here?"

I snap my eyes up when it finally registers what he said as I see Mick walking through the glass front doors. My body locks and freezes wondering what the hell he is doing here. I bite my lip worried he noticed I took all my stuff with me this morning and I'm worried he may cause a scene.

"Hey King," he lifts his chin in greeting. "I need to speak to my sister for a minute," he looks straight at me.

"Step sister," I mumble under my breath before forcing a smile on my face as I push to my feet.

"Sure, why don't we go outside," I say as casually as I can muster as I make my way past him heading straight out the front doors knowing he will follow me.

"What the fuck Mac?" he spits out as soon as the door shuts behind him and I turn to face him on the footpath. I can see the anger as plain as day now that no one else is around and maybe coming out here wasn't such a good idea.

"What's wrong?" I act like I don't know what the hell he's talking about.

"You too fucking good to live with me?" He starts to pace, running his hands wildly through his hair and I wonder why the fuck he's acting like this and I'm not sure what to say to his question without firing him up even more. So, I just shrug my shoulder. I think that was the wrong thing to do when he grabs me by the arm and begins to push his uncut dirty nails into the top of my arm.

"Shit, let go of me," I grit out gripping his hand and bending it back the other way to get him to release me. "Piece of shit don't ever touch me again," I push him off me making him stumble back a step and that's when I notice how wild his eyes are.

Shit is he high?

"Are you fucking him?" he grits out as spit flies from his mouth. I take a step back as the anger in his words hits me in the face. Oh, fuck no, you have got to be kidding me right now. Is he bloody jealous? Disgust runs fast and hard down my spine as bile rises in my throat.

"That's none of your business. Just go home Mick and don't come back." I go to storm past him not wanting to be anywhere near him right now. I knew he was screwed up but this is just messed up I think just as Grayson comes out the doors with a hard look on his face.

"Stupid bitch," Mick spits out at the same time and before I can pass him he swings out and smacks me straight across the face. I hiss out against the sharp sting but before I can kick his ass Grayson shouts out "Son of a bitch," pure rage pouring off him in waves and in a blink of an eye he knocks Mick on his ass in one swing. "Get up you pussy, you think you can touch my woman and get away with it you stupid son of a bitch."

Shit, rubbing my face I quickly race in front of him, putting both my hands up before he kills Mick.

"I'm okay," I repeat over and over till I get his hard eyes on me, blowing out the breath I didn't realise I was holding. He wraps his arms tight around me and his eyes soften, scanning every inch of my face.

"You're coming home with me," he gruffs out not asking but telling me and all I can do is just nod my head against his hard chest feeling his hard breaths start to even out at my agreement.

"Stupid slut, spreading your legs for that piece of shit," Mick groans out trying to get to his feet but my man has other ideas as he kicks him in the guts knocking the wind from him again.

"Piece of shit, one more fucking word and I will end your miserable fucking life," he grunts. His muscles tense ready to kick his ass again.

Turning around in Grayson's hold I look down at Mick writhing like a worm in pain on the ground and nothing but disgust runs through me.

"You ever come near me again you won't have to worry about him kicking your ass 'cause I'll do it myself, you got me you waste of space," I spit out about to take a step forward but Grayson has other ideas and pulls me back into his warm chest and grunts. Turning back into his hold I look up into his smokey green eyes that are swimming with so much possessiveness that a whole new feeling races through me. Reaching up I cup his cheeks running my nails back and forth through his five o'clock shadow.

"I'm okay," I say again trying to reassure him, holding me firm to his chest he bends and kisses the top of my head. My hands slide to the back of his neck at the movement, letting my nails tease the hair on the back of his neck before slipping them back around his waist. Leaning back, I lock eyes with him again, wincing a little in pain when he rubs the pad of his thumb across my cheek. I try to hide it but his nostrils flare and his jaw clenches. So, I guess I didn't hide it very well. His eyes narrow on Mick again above my head who's still whining and moaning in pain on the ground, he goes to move me out of the way but I wrap my arms tighter around his waist, just as Phoenix and Tanner pull into the carpark.

"What's going on brother?" Tanner calls out getting out of a big black SUV.

"This piece of shit thought he could lay his filthy fucking hands on my woman," the vibration of his gruff voice penetrates every cell in my body, squeezing my thighs together as a dull ache begins to build. It only gets worse when Grayson whispers in my ear, "Soon Princess." Running small circles on my lower back with his hand is not helping my situation at all right now either and if his low chuckle is anything to go by he knows exactly what he is doing to me.

"What the fuck," Phoenix spits out snapping me back to reality, shit I thought Phoenix and Tanner were still inside but they must have raced off somewhere. I know they are still trying to track down their latest jumper.

"You hit your fucking sister you piece of shit," Tanner growls out.

"Step," I mumble

"What was that babe?" Grayson asks.

"I'm his step-sister, his dad married my mum, but they got divorced about 2 years ago. His father still cares about me," I mumble the last part and I wonder if Grayson even heard me. I feel his lips on the top of my head before he mumbles that we can talk about it later. I just nod into his chest before I feel warm hands grab me from behind and start to turn me into a warm comforting embrace.

"Come on sweet girl, let's get you inside and let the boys work this out."

"Okay Mrs King," I murmur into her neck as my cheek begins to throb.

"You are now part of this family so no more of this Mrs King crap it's either mum or Tanya that's it."

Nodding I can't stop the soft laugh that slips up my throat.

"Mum take care of my girl," Grayson says worry lacing his tone.

"I'm fine I promise. It was just a shock. I didn't expect it that's all," but he just grunts still not impressed.

"Come on sweetheart let's get you some ice," Tanya says. I smile when I feel his lips hit the top of my head before his mum leads me away.

Seven

Grayson

There would be nothing more satisfying right now then wrapping my hands around this piece of shits neck and watching the life drain from his eyes, but I can't do it. This trash may only be her step-brother but I don't want his death on my hands and mess up any chance I have with my woman.

"What do you wanna do big brother?" Tanner asks chuckling as he kicks Mick in the gut making him choke out a cough.

"Call the cops," I spit out hating the words as they leave my lips.

"You sure brother?" Phoenix asks looking around the empty car park. I watch as a smoldering fire lights up his eyes and I know he wants to bury this prick as much as me. For only being 26 years old Phoenix has already had to deal with a lot of shit and I know that dark part he tries to hide is begging to be released right now.

"Yeah," I blow out a hard breath, running a hand through my hair "just call em and let's get this shit sorted, so I can go see if my girl is okay." Nodding, Tanner pulls his phone out of his pocket and steps away to make the phone call just as Maverick comes out and joins us on the footpath.

"Where you been fucker?" Phoenix slaps him on the back.

"I got a fucking lead on that fuck The Ringmaster, so I was stuck on the fucking phone, looks like you boys could handle this piece of shit without me." He chuckles.

"Fuck. You dickheads will pay for this," Mick groans out.

"Trust me fucker it wouldn't take much to end your miserable life right here and now. So if I was you, I would shut the fuck up." Phoenix gets down low right in the fucks face. Voice low and dark and I watch as the colour drains from Micks face realising how serious Phoenix is right now, and he wisely does as he is told and shuts his mouth.

"Like I said you boys have this shit sorted, I only came out cause otherwise mum would be on my ass about not getting involved," he chuckles pulling a smoke from his pants pocket and lighting it up. Drawing a deep breath he savours the taste then blows it in the direction of Micks face.

"Cops are on the way," Tanner strides over pushing his phone back into his pocket and pulls out his own smokes.

"I thought your girl was gonna rip his head off." Phoenix chuckles, his dark tone from before fading. I just grunt in response not liking the thought of her in the same space as this prick let alone her having to defend herself against him. My body tenses as a thought hits me and a rush on anger flushes through my veins.

"You ever touch her before today?" I grit out between clenched teeth just as a cop car rolls into the carpark. Mick looks between us and the cops with a twisted smirk on his fuck ugly face before locking eyes with me and just winks.

"Motherfucker." I go to take a step forward but Tanners hand on my chest stops me.

"Not worth it brother," he murmurs nodding towards the cops heading our way.

"Fuck this piece of shit," I grunt turning and head back inside.

***

"Mackenzie is fine, she is a lot stronger then she looks," my mother says as soon as I come through the door. Nodding I look over her head towards my girl who's staring at the computer screen in front of her. She must feel my eyes on her cause she looks up and smiles, after a moment she sucks that damn bottom lip into her mouth as her hungry eyes rake over me from head to toe. It's enough to break my control. A deep and burning desire runs through me needing to claim her and make her mine. Fuck I need to pull it back and try to regain my control, there's still work to be done. My brothers would be pissed if I hightailed it out of here with my woman over my shoulder.

"Control son," my father's voice comes from beside me as if reading my mind. I was so zeroed in on my woman I didn't hear his sneaky ass come up beside me. I grunt in response making him chuckle as he shakes his head and heads back to his office with my mother hot on his heels.

"Easy for you to say old man," I call out making him laugh harder.

"Less of the old son, I could still kick your ass," he calls through the open door making me chuckle knowing full well he probably could. I snap my eyes to Mackenzie when her soft laugh floats around me. A deep rumble climbs up my throat watching as her little pink tongue

46

swipes across her bottom lip and her hungry eyes seem to be caressing every single inch of my body. My cock pushes against my zipper and I know I have to stop her wandering eyes before I take her on the desk in front of her and say fuck it. Jealousy pure and raw rages through me at the thought of someone else hearing her moans of pleasure. They're mine and nobody will ever hear them besides me.

Making my way towards her desk I come up behind her needing to touch her and make sure she is okay.

"Are you okay babe?" Resting my hands on her shoulders I rub my thumbs around the back of her neck feeling her melt into my hold. My pulse kicks up a notch at just this simple touch. Bending I bury my nose into the top of her hair breathing in her sweet scent. A soft moan leaves her lips making a low growl slip up my throat at the sound. *Fuck.*

"Really, I'm fine," she all but purrs out and reflexively I squeeze her shoulders feeling the shiver race through her at my hard touch.

Interesting.

Leaning her head back, I plant a kiss to her forehead and watch as her eyes flutter shut.

"G man the cops wanna talk to you and Mac," Mav's annoying voice cuts through our moment. Not paying him any attention my lips linger on her silky soft skin needing just another moment.

"We should go talk to them," Mackenzie murmurs. Nodding I let her up. Taking her hand in mine I lead her out the front. I look up and see Maverick smirking.

"Pussy whipped," he murmurs under his breath as we go to pass him making Mackenzie giggle. Fucking asshole. I elbow him in the gut making him grunt. I can't wait for the day a woman has him so tightly wound around her finger and has him begging for the slightest bit of attention. Just having Mackenzie in my space is enough to stabilize something deep inside me I didn't even know was off balance. That connection I felt the minute I saw her only seems to get stronger.

"You wait, fucker," I mumble making him laugh while he rubs the spot I just elbowed.

"Not gonna happen, brother."

"Come on Caveman," Mackenzie sasses out pulling me by the hand towards the door. Not looking back at Mav, I pull Mackenzie back into my chest and wrap my arms around her waist. Bending I latch onto her earlobe with my teeth, nipping her before sucking the stinging flesh into my mouth. A shudder races through her body like wildfire and I smile against the smooth skin of her neck loving how she responds to me.

"Keep that sass up princess, cause' I'm gonna enjoy fucking it right out of you," I whisper low so only she can hear watching as goosebumps break out. Looking over her shoulder she locks eyes with me and I swear I see nervousness swim in those honey eyes but it's gone just as fast as it came. A mischievous smile spreads across her face.

Eight

Mackenzie

"He's gone underground, there is nothing more we can do until my informant gets back to me," Tanner says frustration coating his words as he paces back and forth between the desks.

"How the fuck did he know we were onto him, to begin with?" Phoenix pipes in from across the room. "I bet ya 10 bucks your informant." Phoenix does air quotes when he says informant and I have to bite my lip from laughing as he follows it up with an eye roll. A snort slips free and I quickly tuck my chin into my chest before anyone hears me but I'm guessing I'm too late when a low growl from beside me pulls my attention to Grayson. A light chuckle leaves Phoenix's mouth from in front of my desk as heat rushes up my neck spreading throughout my cheeks. I throw Grayson a wink, trying to act like his growling isn't affecting me. But in all honesty, I have to squeeze my thighs together under the desk to try and dull the ache that seems to be there since meeting the giant of a man. As if knowing my thoughts, a sexy smirk kicks up the side of his mouth. My eyes seemed to be drawn to the motion and I suck my bottom lip into my mouth remembering the taste of him from earlier. Running his tongue across his bottom lip I press my teeth harder into my own to stop the moan that wants to slip free just as he mouths the word mine. I'm about ready to combust, closing my eyes I take in a few shallow breaths, as my heart echoes in my ears.

"Is a lying piece of shit," Phoenix finishes snapping my attention back to the conversation and I feel like I need to thank him for the distraction. A small smile kisses my lips when Nix as his brothers call him turns and winks at me, pissing Grayson off even more.

"Cut the shit Nix before I break your face, she's mine," his voice takes on a low deep quality that sends shivers racing down my spine and has me squirming in my seat.

"Well, I guess they don't call him The Ringmaster for nothing," Maverick breaks in shrugging his shoulders with his eyes still glued to his computer screen. Completely not phased that Grayson wants to beat up their brother. Since the police left earlier this morning, we have been running up leads to find The Ringmaster but so far, we have come up empty. Every lead seems people don't know who we are talking about or they are just too scared to give up anything and so far with my own research I have discovered he has a long reach. He wouldn't hesitate to hurt anybody that spoke up about where to find him.

"Let me take you home," his deep whisper floats down my neck startling me a little not even hearing him move. His hands land against my shoulders, his thumbs moving in a slow agonizing motion up my neck till he reaches my pulse points. Sucking in a lungful of air as liquid heat rushes through every one of my veins and heads directly to my clit, a small gasp leaves my lips. A vibration bone-deep chases through me as if it's trying to catch up with the heat. Dropping my head, I take in lungfuls of air trying to calm my ass down. There is no way he won't notice the heat flushing through my cheeks once again. I need a goddamn minute to let my head catch up with my body. Shaking my head at the thought knowing I would end up being a puddle of need at his feet. How is it that this man can make me putty in his hands with the smallest of words or the simplest of touches? Am I that desperate for a guy to touch me that the first guy that does sends my body into a frenzy wishing that he would never stop? I gnaw on my bottom lip as a new worry swims through my head at ramped speed. Shit, how am I going to tell him that I have never let a guy touch me? Will he think I'm too innocent and push me aside? Would he be worried that I would become a stage 5 clinger if we ever had sex or would he beat his chest like a brute, proud to be my first?

"Hey, where did you go?" A light tug on my bottom lip pulls me back to the moment and he must have turned my chair around without me noticing as I look into scorching green eyes that seem to darken by the second and see straight to my very soul. Mustering up a smile I try to calm my anxiety about whether I would be just another conquest and once he is done taking what he obviously wants he will throw me away. I know I come off like I have my shit together but, in all honesty, this day with him has me off kilter and I don't know what to think. He speaks as if I'm claimed property and I know I should be smacking him across the face. But I can't stop the thrill that shoots through me every time he calls me his.

"Huh?" I answer him taking in a few deep breaths, the air burning my lungs as my mind goes over so many different scenarios. I need to figure all this shit out and fast. Going back to my step-brother's place isn't a damn option so a motel it is. I need to break the intense gaze, pull and hold that Grayson has on me enough for me to think clearly and get my shit together.

"Princess," his voice floats over me as he puts his strong hands on either side of my face and pulls me into him his eyes burning into my core. "I um... I'm fine." I stutter out into his eyes blinking and looking away I don't want him to see the worry and the doubt in my eyes.

"I got you, Princess, no matter what you're safe with me." Melting into him tears brim at my eyes. Fuck my body is a traitor.

"I wanna run," I blurt out his body instantly goes tense. Oh my, his jaw clenches and I swear that I heard it snap. Fire laces his eyes and my skin ripples in a shudder instantly regretting what I just said. Fuck the honesty is the best policy isn't going so well especially when I just blurt that shit out.

"What!" Grayson's tone is thick causing me to jump in his grip that only tightens around me.

"This is all too much, too fast." I blurt out again.

Leaping from my seat I run out the front door before he has a chance to say another word. But before I can hit the second step his strong arms are around me lifting me off my feet and I'm over his shoulder. "You ain't running away from me Princess." His gravelly tone has a hard edge that vibrates over my body and a chill leaps down my spine. Before I can even form a reply a stinging hits my ass and I have to bite my lip to stop a moan from slipping free. My body shivers as he begins to rub the sting away. What the hell was that all about? I should be kicking and screaming. Demanding he let me go but my traitorous body has other ideas and seems to mold into his shoulder and my ass pushes into his hand. As if silently begging for more.

"Interesting." He murmurs so low I'm lucky to catch it but I do and I try to stop the small whimper that slips up my throat but it's no use.

"We are going to go outside and talk about this and then I'm going to tell you all the reasons you leaving me is not fucking happening," he grunts.

"I'm a messed up hot mess," I mumble as he begins to slide me down the front of his body and I bite back a groan as I feel every hard edge on the man. My feet touch the ground and my back hits something solid. Looking over my shoulder I realise I'm against my car but I have no room to turn and jump in as he pushes into me that I have no choice but to spread my legs a little. His fingers flex against my curved hips as he rests them there. Looking up into his strong face I suck in a deep breath at the hard set of his eyes.

"I'm sorry," I blurt out. Lifting his hand, he places a finger over my lips to stop me from talking. I narrow my eyes at the motion making him chuckle.

"Fuck babe, you make my head spin."

My back stiffens at his words.

"Well maybe…"

"My turn to talk Princess," he cuts me off.

"From the first moment I saw you yesterday you have set my head spinning, to the point where work and all the other bullshit doesn't matter. The only thing that matters is you, everything else is just a meaningless backdrop," he pauses blowing out a hard breath before continuing. "I know we only just met but we have forever to get to know each other. Right here, right now tell me you don't feel this connection between us," he dares me and as much as I should say I don't feel it I can't bring myself to lie to him. I do feel it, I feel it so deep that the thought alone consumes my mind, jolts my body like electricity.

"I feel it," I murmur staring at his chest, I feel the tips of his fingers slip underneath my chin pulling my face up to his, as my eyes connect with his. Liquid heat begins to travel straight through me as the hungry look in his eyes seem to devour every single cell in my body. Licking my lips, I suck in a shaky breath wanting to taste him, feel the movement of his body as it slides against mine. How does he do that? One minute I'm scared to open myself up worried I would mean nothing to him once he saw how screwed up I really am and the next I want everything he has to offer. His words spark an inferno raging through me and all I want is to wrap myself around this man and let him love me.

Holy shit! Did I just say love? Do I love him?

Gripping Grayson's shoulders, my nails bite into the hard muscle as I bow my head so my forehead rests against his hard chest. Sucking in lungfuls of air as the realisation hits me square in the chest. When he looks at me it's as if every ounce of breath is taken from my lungs floating into the air like midnight smoke. Every time he kisses me it feels like the world stops, leaving just the two of us to wander the earth together. Every time he holds my face between his hands it feels like he is untying all of my knots. If this is what falling in love is like, I want it. It's time to rewrite my own story and get the happy ending I have always dreamed about and this is the one story I never want to end. For so long I have longed for this, and now I can't bear to lose it - lose this thing that makes me feel so complete. As much as it's a strange feeling – frightening even – how can we go from being complete strangers, to then being completely infatuated by them and wondering how it ever was that you were able to live without them. Because you sure as shit couldn't imagine being without them now. I feel the rough touch of his hand as he slides it up my back until he reaches my hair, wrapping his fingers between the strands he gives them a little tug getting my attention so I lift my eyes to his. Leaning down he places a quick kiss on my lips before pulling back.

"No running Princess," he breathes out and all I can do is nod. "I need you in my life babe. Just stay with me, give **this** a chance and I will prove to you every day that I want you and only you," his deep voice whispers above my lips and I catch the small plea that lines his words as they squeeze my heart.

"Okay."

"Yeah," a sensual smile creeps over his handsome face and I can't help but laugh.

"Prove to me we can make this work," I breathe out cupping the sides of his face. "I'm with you one hundred percent," I choke out tasting the truth to my own words making my heart stutter in my chest at the realisation that I have fallen head over heels in love with this man and whether it's 1 week, a year or forever I will be beside him as long as he will have me.

"Let me take you home Princess," he breathes out as he slides his lips across mine sending a whole new sensation running through me.

Nine

Grayson

Jumping in my truck, kicking the car over, the engine thunders to life as I watch the cherry red Cadillac reverse out of her spot. It then pulls to the driveway of the carpark and idles while she waits for me to go in front. Rolling past her I can't stop the chuckle rumbling up my throat as *Cream by Prince* blasts through her speakers. Fuck she's sexy, sassy and cute as hell but she still has this air of innocence that surrounds her that has every one of my protective instincts kicking into gear, wanting nothing more than to hide her away from the rest of the world so nothing ever touches her again. There is something so captivating and soulful in her eyes that the thought of never having her with me tears at my heart. She is a flicker of a flame in the dead of night leading you home. An ache settles in my chest and I flatten my palm there trying to rub it away. Looking out my rearview mirror before I exit the car park. Her fingers tap against the steering wheel as that plump mouth of hers sings along to the music. Dark raven hair highlighted with blonde streaks dances around her as it catches on the wind. It's like I'm caught in a spell and I can't pull my eyes away. Taking a deep breath in the faint smell of coconut and lime lingers around the enclosed space, without pulling my eyes away from the mirror I lift my shirt to my nose, rumbling low in my throat as the scent gets stronger. The sound of a horn makes me realise I closed my eyes. Snapping my eyes towards the mirror again my chest seems to constrict at the saucy smile pulling at her lips and I choke out a breath as a feeling so consuming begins to make my head spin.

Oh, shit do I love her? But how? When?

These overwhelming emotions are so strange; they stretch throughout my whole body. It's overwhelming, yet it makes me feel complete. There are no bounds or lengths nor depth; it's just there and absolute.

"Fuck I love her," I gasp out. As the words leave my mouth, I taste the very truth of my words on my tongue as a hole I didn't know I had inside me begins to heal. 48 hours that's all it took for this sexy, curvy slip of a woman to bring me to my knees and fuck if I can't wait to get her under me screaming my name for the rest of the world to hear.

***

My place is only a ten-minute drive from Bounty King's in Adamstown. Today though that ten-minute car ride felt like a lifetime. My palms were sweaty and my heart beating some strange ass beat that it had never done before. I found myself constantly looking in the rearview mirror of my truck watching for my girl. Afraid that she would turn off and run. Fuck I get that this is a fast ass thing that's happening with us both but fuck this instant love shit hits you fast and hard. A low chuckle leaves my throat realising how true my father's words have been all my life. This shit grips onto every nerve in your body and refuses to let go and I know no matter what I will never let her slip through my fingers. I know she feels what I feel and I'll spend the rest of my fucking days proving to her that she's it for me. Fuck I get why she is scared and wanting to run cause these feelings scare the shit out of me too. But losing her scares me even more so I will do everything in my power to keep her till the end of fucking time and I will make sure that cocksucker step-brother of hers pays for today's stunt. My grip tightens on the steering wheel just thinking about that fuck. Blowing out a hard breath I try to relax back in my seat, flexing my fingers against the steering wheel, feeling the rush of blood as it makes its way back into the tips of my fingers knowing Mick is behind a set of metal bars right now. I have this feeling deep down in the pit of my stomach that he won't be gone for long and if he does have the balls to come at my girl again, I will bury him six feet under and not give two shits about it. Knowing my girl is safe will be enough to take that pricks life.

Flicking my eyes towards the rearview mirror again I can't help but laugh as my eyes meet hers watching her singing and dancing like no one's watching, stuck in her own little bubble. Fuck me she's beautiful. Taking the left turn onto my street, I push the accelerator a bit more to get up the hill my place sits on top of at the end of the street. Slowing down I pull up into my driveway. My home isn't the typical bachelor pad besides the rough outside inside it's fucking clean and crisp. I'm never here so I have no time to make a mess. Pulling up tight to the side of my house making sure there is enough space for her to park next to me I glance to my right as she pulls up hard beside me. Killing my engine I can't help but chuckle as her music blares from her car. Shit, how are her ears not bleeding right now? She's definitely something else alright and she's all fucking mine. Stepping from the truck I stride over to her side of the car, opening her door I pull her from the car and into my chest. Her scent hits me straight away and my cock strains against the zipper of my pants loving the feeling of her so close. Her giggle floats around us at the sudden movement and it's music to my fucking ears. Her cheeks pinken a little as her body moulds to mine feeling the hardness, her eyes quickly dart to the ground but not before I see the apprehension flash through them. I sense that there is more to her then she is letting on and by the end of the night I hope I can crack her wide open enough to let me in.

Leaning down I bury my nose into the top of her hair breathing in her scent. "Let's go inside Princess and have a drink," I gruff out knowing the last thing on my mind is a drink but I need to take this slow as not to scare her. Picking her up around the waist, her smooth legs automatically wrap around me.

"I can walk," she breathes out against my neck. "I got you babe," I murmur loving the feeling of her in my arms. She just feels so right, So mine. Carrying her up the few steps I wrap one arm under her ass and hold her to me as I fish out my keys in my pocket. Turning the locks, I lean down kissing her temple wanting to tell her this is her new home now but after her wanting to run earlier I worry it may freak her out. So instead, I move through the doorway, kicking it shut behind me with the heel of my boot and head towards the kitchen dropping her down on the counter as I go about making us both a whiskey on ice. Placing a glass in her tiny hands I notice that they seem to be shaking slightly.

"Sorry Princess, whiskey is all I got." I say looking into her eyes. "It's ok, I don't mind." Her voice fills the empty walls of my home and bounce back hitting me hard in the chest. Shit, it feels good having my woman's voice lace the space between us and now I realise that's been the missing part to my puzzle all along.

"Come on let's sit out back and watch the sunset," I say to her picking up on her nerves that are fucking making me nervous. Pushing the glass bi-fold doors open I pick up the small blanket off the back of the chair and wrap it over her shoulders as she sits down. "It's beautiful out here," she says sipping slowly on her drink as I down mine in one massive gulp. "Sure is," I crunch out as my teeth crack down on the ice cubes but my focus isn't on the view it's completely zeroed in on her as the sun seems to shine behind her making a halo effect.

"So, Princess what's going on in that beautiful head of yours?" I question as her eyes find mine

"It's okay you can tell me anything and believe me I won't run," I say to her on the chance that she can hear the truth in my words as I speak. Her eyes leave mine and look out over the world below us. The tree tops are full of bird song as the sun starts to kiss goodnight to the moon. Watching her suck in a deep soul searching breath "Well, I...um...mmm, well shit," she stutters out and I try not to chuckle at the sudden shyness that washes over her. Her cheeks are red and it looks fucking hot on her sun blushed complexion, her midnight hair falls and shields the side her face. Reaching over I tuck the silky strands behind her ear letting the tips over my fingers slide down the curve of her smooth cheek.

"I'm a virgin," she blurts out and hides her face in her hands. Fuck me if that wasn't the hottest thing I have ever fucking heard. My head spins for the hundredth time today as her words register and a primal need to mark her as mine for the world to see washes through me. Clearing my throat, I try to hide the roughness of my voice. "Well Princess," I manage to choke out, reaching forward I run the tips of my fingers lightly under her chin feeling the shiver that races through her from my touch. Lifting her face to mine her honey eyes meet mine worry and embarrassment lacing them.

"That means you will be mine in every way," I husk out as her mouth pops open in shock and a million emotions swim through those captivating eyes of hers. Running my thumb across her bottom lip, a small gasp slips free causing a low growl to rumble in my chest. "You're mine," I push out and all she does is nod her eyes not leaving mine. Well, not like I give her a chance as the grip of my fingers on her chin hold her gaze in place with mine. "I will be your first and your fucking last. I will show you just how much a man can worship one woman's fucking body." She swallows hard as I slide my fingers lightly down her throat as her shaking hands down the rest of her drink, running my thumb lightly down the centre of her throat feeling her throat work as the smooth whiskey slides down. My hand falls from her neck taking the glass from her hands. Sliding one hand into the back of her head, my fingers twist in the silky strands there holding her still at the base of her skull. My lips find hers taking her sweet soul in one hard fast passionate kiss. Wrapping her small body into mine I lift her up growling lowly as her body moulds into mine so perfectly that I would be a fucking fool to not realise this woman was mine. Carrying her to my room, I kick the door closed with my booted foot never releasing her lips from mine. Bending at the waist I lay her flat on the bed as my lips slide down her neck, nipping at her collarbone, her breaths pick up as I travel back up feeling her pulse point jump rapidly under the assault of my lips, sucking her there for a moment before pulling back with a small pop, my heart beats faster in my chest at the sight of the small red mark I left there. "I'm gonna mark every flawless inch of your sexy as fuck body and have you begging for more. By the time I am done there won't be any doubt in your head who you belong to Princess," I growl low as I lean back ripping my shirt over my head. Her eyes track the movement as a small gasp leaves her parted lips, her chest moving rapidly as she takes in every detail on display for her.

"I want to mark you too," she fucking purrs sending the primal beast inside me racing to the surface wanting her to mark me. Bracing my knees on the end of the bed I fall forward placing my hands either side of her head, taking a moment to breathe in her sweet scent.

"Your first time shouldn't be rough and dirty but all I can think about is binding your pretty little hands to my bed and have you begging for release as sweat drips down the curves of your body and your heartbeat is echoing in my ears as your heated breaths are rushing out of you while you try to scream my name." I murmur low in her ear as her body shudders from the vibration of my voice, her chest rises and falls faster, making her hard nipples press into my chest on each exhale. I feel the motion of her trying to squeeze her legs together but preventing her from any kind of comfort I push my leg between hers stopping the movement. A deep rumble crawls up my throat as the heat of her wet pussy presses against my thigh. A moan slips up her pretty throat when I apply a little pressure. Her head tilts back slightly and I can't help running the tips of my fingers over the sensual curve.

"Please," she gasps.

"Please what princess?" my voice comes out hoarse with the heat of my own arousal.

"Anything, everything," she rushes out tilting her hips up just a bit more.

"Maybe if I tied you up you can't run from me anymore."

"I...I promise not to run from you," she stutters. Her heated breath rushing over me and if I wasn't already so attuned to her, I think that voice alone with the way it seems to smooth over all my hard edges would be enough to have me begging for even the tiniest bit of scrap she has to offer. I gently lay my hand against her neck giving a little squeeze feeling her pulse race out of control and her eyes half close. "Fuck, you like that idea princess." Not even trying to hide the gruffness of my voice. All she seems to manage in reply is a slight nod of her head. Her little pink tongue swipes across her bottom lip making it hard to resist slamming my mouth on hers.

"Naked now," I demand pushing off the bed and standing at my full height watching as firstly she uses one heel to kick off her shoe before the other follows suit. Reaching over I grip her ankles, the heat from her skin seems to sear through me as I take her socks off one by one before leveling her feet back on the bed so she can get her pants off. I bite off a growl when I notice her scarlet red toenails curl into the gray bedcover. Never in my life have I thought feet were sexy but something about the splash on red against her sun blushed skin has my already hard cock begging for release. Letting my eyes take in her shaky hands she pops the button just as she slides the fly down and the sound seems to echo around us mingling with our heavy breathing. Tilting my head I study the perfect curve of her face as a mischievous glint shines from the honey depths of her eyes and I bite my lip to stop the smirk curling to the side wondering what she's up to.

"I may be a virgin but that doesn't mean I don't have some tricks up my sleeve Player," her voice is husky laden with a thick sex operator voice that has a deep growl sliding up my throat and I can't take my eyes away from the show she is putting on for me. Arching her back her legs slide up the bed till they rest about 30 centimeters away from her ass. She slides both hands under her shirt, taking the shirt with her at the movement cupping both her breasts in her hands a small whimper leaves her pretty lips. The sight just about has me losing my load and I haven't even touched her. Grunting I go to take a step towards the end of the bed but a husky tsking sound snaps my eyes to hers. Her raven hair is spread out like a fan around her, her lips slightly parting as shallow breaths puff out but that's not what has my body wanting to spring into action. Her eyelids have slid to half-mast and are laden with so many promises it has the air leaving my lungs in a rush as one hand slides down the front of her open pants. A slight whimper escapes her lips again and I can't pull my eyes away from the way her wrist starts a slow circular motion. It takes everything in me to turn my back and head towards my chest of drawers sliding the top drawer open I look over my shoulder as another low husky moan echoes behind me.

"Fuck," I mutter as those lust, soul filled honey eyes lock with mine again.

"You want to play Princess?" I manage to get through the pounding racing through me and I don't even try to stop the low chuckle coming out when I pull out the red rope from my top drawer and let it hang from my fingers. I listen as her breaths seem to skip a beat before picking up the pace and the hand that's still circling her hard clit in her pants seems to pick up speed at the same time. Her other hand gripping her breast starts pinching her nipple and my mouth waters wanting that hard nub in my mouth. Looking back to her eyes again seeing the slight hesitation but it's gone as quick as it comes as a sexual need ignites seeming to spark the space between us.

"You want to play Princess?" I repeat my earlier question noticing how deep and scratchy my voice has become.

"I.." she stops to lick her lips making me growl lowly "I want you anyway I can," she murmurs fire and shyness taking over her words and I don't know how it's possible to make that sentence sexy as fuck but she does. Wrapping the rope over my shoulders I turn back to the bed taking up the space between us in a heartbeat. Before she even has time to react, I reach over gripping the top of her jeans and panties pulling them off in one swift go. Her squeak of surprise leaves her lips but before she can utter a protest or try to hide from me, I lean forward nudging her hand out of the way bury my face in her bare wet flesh. Growling at her taste as it coats my tongue, I run my hands up her smooth body till I'm cupping her breasts. I weigh them while pinching her tight nipples till her body is completely lost to the pleasure, pain running through her veins.

"Shit," her murmured breath comes out as her fingers slide through my hair. A shiver races through me hard and fast as her nails scrape across my scalp before she begins to twist the ends of my hair between her fingers. Sucking her hard clit into my mouth I bite down a little feeling her body stiffen as her thighs begin to close around my head. Turning my head slightly I nip the sweet flesh on the inside of her thigh making her jerk her legs back open. Sliding one hand down the middle of her chest her breaths coming heavy as her skin quivers under my touch. Slowly I slide one finger inside her hot wet heat and I can't stop the growl slipping free when her tight muscles begin squeezing around the digit. She is so tight I struggle to push my finger in all the way.

"Fuck babe," I grunt trying to push another finger inside her after a few taps to her hard as fuck clit I lean over and suck her hard nipple in my mouth. The taste of her pussy paired with the taste of coconut on my tongue has all my senses firing and my balls drawing up tight to my body. Squeezing my eyes shut I fight off the urge to cum as her body relaxes slightly enough so I can push another finger inside her dripping pussy.

"Ahhh..." she cries out in a smooth husky voice. Looking at her as her head tilts back her back arching more making her nipple rub against the roof of my mouth, I curl my fingers and move them in a come-hither motion hitting that spot that will send her flying over the edge.

"Cum," I clip watching as pure passion and ecstasy rolls over her features. A sheen of sweat coats her skin as I strum my thumb over her clit prolonging her orgasm. I feel the slight tremors racing through her and never before have I ever witnessed something so sexy. Releasing her nipple with a small pop I grunt in satisfaction at the puckered red nub. 1 mark down 100 more to go I think as I grip the rope around my neck leaning back on my knees, removing my fingers from the vice like grip she has on them, sucking them into my mouth I growl around the flavor not wanting to waste a drop. Leaning over I pull her shirt over her head before gripping both her slim wrists and securing them to the wooden panels of my bed head. Leaning down I plant a kiss to her nose then her lips, sliding my tongue across her bottom lip so she can taste herself on me. I growl when she moans sucking on my tongue.

Sitting back on my heels I run the tips of my fingers down her sides watching as goosebumps break out across her flawless skin. Not flawless for long I think to myself as I push from the bed and that's when her liquid honey eyes begin to flicker open showing that sex drunk look that has my insides jack knifing through me. Testing her arms, she looks back and realises what I have done and a look crosses her face I don't understand. Just when I think she may not be into it and I get ready to untie her she arches again. "Show me what ya got Player," that sex operator voice smooths out again smashing me in the chest and begins to beat out a tune loud and thundering in my ears. Fuck who would believe she's a fucking virgin with the things coming out of that sensual mouth that seems to drip with every fantasy I have ever had.

Kicking off my boots, I snap open my belt and the sound seems to echo around us, flipping my button open I slip my fly down releasing some of the pressure around my hard cock. Pushing my pants off I lean down taking my socks off never taking my eyes off the vixen in my bed, our bed. Fuck that sounds good. Grunting with the thought I lean back rubbing my throbbing cock at the sight of her tied up and ready for the taking. Letting my eyes slide from the red rope binding her to our bed I watch as her little tongue swipes across her lips again as her eyes are locked on what my hand is doing. Possessiveness rushes through me hot and fast and as much as I want to take my time with her and worship every single inch of pure untouched skin, I know I need to get inside her and mark her as mine. With her legs slightly parted I see the wetness from her desire coating her thighs and I can't stop myself from leaning down and having another taste.

"So sweet," I murmur as her low moan and the quiver of her thighs runs through me. Locking my eyes with hers and before I can catch the words they pour from my lips.

"Are you on the pill?" I grunt feeling my muscles tense waiting for her answer. A look of disappointment washes over her face before she shakes her head and the clamp like grip running through my muscle's releases.

"Good," I grunt. A surprised look splashes over her face taking away the disappointment from seconds before.

"G-good," she stutters.

"Fuck yeah Princess," I crawl up the bed. Her legs automatically wrapping around my waist. I groan feeling the wet heat from her pussy soak through my briefs and I flex into her making her moan pushing up to rub herself against my hard cock and I have to grit my teeth against the pleasure.

"I'm taking you bare," I manage to hoarse out. "Then no one would ever doubt you are mine," I lay a hand over her soft belly just thinking how sexy she would look round with my baby. Never in my life have I thought about having kids but right now the need to breed with her chases down my spine and making my head spin with satisfaction.

"W-what?" she stutters before licking her lips and locking her eyes with mine a million emotions swim through the bright orbs "But what if.." I don't let her finish the sentence before swooping down and claiming her lips in a hard kiss.

"I can't think of anything sexier than you round with my baby," I push out when I pull back from the kiss "A little girl with dark raven hair and honey eyes," I murmur running the tips of my fingers down the side of her face. A shuddering breath rushes out of her parted lips hitting me in the face as a light sparks in the depths of her eyes.

"You want to have a baby with me?" It comes out a whisper but I hear the hope in her voice.

"I want everything with you Princess."

"Well damn," she breathes out as a sexy grin curves her lips making me chuckle. Her legs flex around me and I automatically push into her. Kissing her one more time I push back breaking the hold of her legs as a sound of protest escapes her lips. A gasp quickly follows it as I push my briefs off in one fluid motion. Her fingers flex around the bindings before gripping them tight as her body arches at the motion kicking my briefs to the side, I crawl back up the bed her soft body sliding against mine. A soft mewling sound slips up her throat as my hard cock lays across her wet pussy as precum slides across her lower belly my body locks at the sight and I growl low in the back of my throat as I begin to rub it into her soft skin. Lifting my fingers, I tap her bottom lip as her tongue comes out to taste me. Humming around the digits she looks up at me through her lashes.

"I want more," she begs.

"Soon Princess," I promise knowing if her mouth gets anywhere near my cock right now, I won't be able to hold back from shooting cum down her pretty throat.

Gripping the base of my cock I swipe back and forth through her wetness gritting my teeth against the pleasure as she begins to rock against me. It's the sweetest torture I have ever known. Locking my jaw, my nose flares as I push the first inch in slowly. My eyes cross feeling her tightness, a tightness I have never felt before. I don't want to cause her any pain, leaning forward a bit more I watch as my cock disappear a little more. Pulling my eyes away from our connection before I lose all control I lean over and capture her lips in a deep kiss, gripping my fingers with hers I thrust all the way in and capture the small whimper that escapes her lips as I break through her innocence. That feeling of possessiveness beats down on me harder knowing she is mine and nobody will ever have the privilege of feeling her tight as fuck pussy wrap around them. The caveman inside me wants to beat his chest knowing she is mine and nobody can take her away from me. Pulling my lips from hers I kiss her closed lids and lick up the single tear that slips past her lashes.

"I'm sorry Princess," I groan out as her muscles squeezing my cock in a death grip and I can't stop myself from cumming a little bit coating her virgin walls.

"I need you to move," she grounds out as her eyes flick to mine, her legs wrap tight around my waist pulling me deeper and I feel her throbbing pussy against every ridge of my cock as I slowly start to pull out.

"Fuck," I grunt pushing back in.

"Yes" she moans as her fingers squeeze mine.

Releasing my hold on her hands I grip her hips tight. Leaning back I start up a slow pace thrusting in and out. I grit my teeth against the wet heat of her pussy as it slides against me.

"Faster," she pants. That one word has my control snapping in two and I can't hold back anymore. Thrust after agonizing thrust my speed picks up. Leaning down capturing her hard nipple in my mouth applying a little pressure with my teeth I grunt as her pussy contracts around me. Her legs tense, her mouth opens on a scream of my name and it's the sexiest sound I have ever heard. Sweat slicks against both our skin as I continue to pump in and out needing her to cum one more time before I let go. Reaching up I release both her hands from the bindings wanting her touch.

"Again Princess," I growl.

She opens her mouth probably to protest but as I thrust back in her eyes widen as the feeling of her first release slides down my balls.

"Grayson," she moans as her nails score down my back and the bite of her nails has me slamming into her harder. I clutch her hair in a fist, angling her mouth so I can take it in a bruising kiss feeling her body surrendering to me. The power of owning this vixen is a heady feeling and I know no matter what I will never get enough. Just as the thought crosses my mind her muscles tense, she arches, her head pulls back from the kiss on a scream. Pushing as deep as I can go, I let go letting my orgasm consume me as my cum coats her flawless virgin pussy. Running my hands across her belly my chest tightens with the thought I just got her pregnant and I can't stop the smile spreading over my lips.

"You look pretty pleased with yourself Player," she exhales on a deep husky breath and I hear the teasing in her voice.

"I love you Princess," I husk out. "I know we just met but I knew you are supposed to be mine from the minute I saw you," I rush out worried my words may frighten her. Locking my eyes with hers so she can see the truth of my words. Her eyes glass over making the honey colour look like liquid and I worry that I have scared her but after a moment of silence besides our panting breaths she sets my body on fire all over again.

"I love you too Player."

And just like that the loneliness I have always felt drifts away and a warmth of need settles in its place. My cock twitches inside her tight pussy and her muscles flex around me making me groan. Pulling out I groan at the loss of her tight heat. Flipping her over I pull her hips up and bury my cock to the hilt making her groan out in pleasure. Lifting my hand, I do what I have wanted to do since I have seen her bent over the hood of her car. Spanking her ass 3 times I growl as I rub the spot as her ass pushes against my hand wanting more.

"Sexy as fuck babe. Now reach up to the headboard and hang on."

"Yes Sir," she moans automatically and those words set a fire off inside of me.

"Fuck," I grunt out as her small giggle turns into a moan as I begin to thrust. Being in this position I know I won't last long especially with the way her pussy is gripping me but I can hit deeper this way and when I come it's going to shoot directly into her womb. I whisper all this into her ear and she ignites and begins to push harder against me matching me in every thrust.

"You make sure you suck every drop out of me with that greedy pussy of yours Princess," I grunt out one hand wrapped through her hair while I wrap one around her waist and begin to rub her hard clit.

"Give me what I want Princess," I growl pistoning my hips as her body begins to tense up.

"Fuck, cum." I yank her back against me as the beginning of her orgasm hits her and she calls out my name sucking every drop of cum from me. Laying her forward into the soft bed I lift her hips up as a soft whimper leaves her parted lips.

"Rest Princess but we are far from done," I murmur running my hands down her back as I slowly keep thrusting in and out. By the time we have finished she is not gonna know how to walk and she will be bred with my baby.

Ten

Mackenzie

I'm startled awake by the sound of a phone going off. I groan and bury myself back into Grayson's warmth, stretching a little. I can't stop the whispered moan slipping up my throat as I ache from the way he devoured me all night. Or it could have been only an hour ago. My brain is a puddle of satisfaction right now that I don't even know what time it is. Grayson's sleepy husky voice vibrates through me as he speaks into the phone and it's enough to nearly lull me back to sleep until the next words leave his mouth and he pushes up from the bed. My eyes fly open and my nerves on a razor's edge as my body moves with his. A small shiver races through me as Grayson's hand runs up and down my back trying to comfort me as well as him, I suppose, as a tension so strong locks his body. Placing my hand against his thigh I give it a small rub and feel him relax just a fraction.

"Mum calm down. What happened?" he bites out pausing a moment listening to his mum.

"Fuck we will be there in 20," he finishes ending the call.

"Princess we have to go, my brother, has been shot," as he clips out the words I'm already out of bed and pulling his t-shirt over my head as I look around for my pants not giving two shits what I look like right now.

The chill of the early morning air hits me and goosebumps ripple over my arms and down my spine. My mind is racing as I think of the what's, who's, and why this has happened. Feeling guilty for leaving and relishing in Grayson's body and just how capable he is. He hurries us to his truck his body in full panic mode and before I can even shut the truck door he is reversing out the driveway and speeding down the road. Coming up to the stop sign I finally have clipped my seatbelt in and we are heading rather fast in the direction of the hospital. Grayson is murmuring under his breath.

"I'm sorry," I blurt out. "If it wasn't for me you would have been with him." It's then I realize tears are streaming down my face as the bite of the cold air from Grayson's open window cools the drops. I jump a little as I feel the warmth of his hand as it slides over mine and giving it a small squeeze. I expect him to pull his hand away but he doesn't and instead, he laces our fingers together.

"Princess this isn't your fault," he blows out a hard breath as he slows for the red light ahead.

"That fuck The Ringmaster is at fault and that fucker better run cause' if I catch him, he is as good as dead," he vows a deadly edge to his voice.

"But if…" I stammer out.

"Babe we had no leads to where this fuck was so you don't get to shoulder this guilt you feel. Wherever my brother found this cocksucker it wasn't on purpose so until then we wait to find out what the fuck happened."

I mull over his words and I know what he is saying is true and I just hope to hell his brother is okay. We fall silent as Grayson takes the dark roads towards the hospital and all I can hope is his brother isn't critical.

"I know my brother babe, and he wouldn't chase down a lead by himself," he grunts out pulling me from my thoughts. I look around noticing we have pulled into the carpark at the hospital and I'm amazed at how quick we got here and at how empty the lot is. Swinging my attention to the clock on the dashboard I realize it's 4 am, no wonder it's empty apart from a handful of cars scattered around...

Rushing past the night security heading towards ED we don't get a chance to ask where we need to go as Tanya rushes out a set of double doors and intercepts us.

"Son! God, am I glad to see you. Tanner..." Tanya hiccups her voice a crack above full hysteria. Grayson pulls her into his massive arms engulfing her tiny body and running his hand down her back. He is so calming and just amazing and all he cares about right now is calming his mum, making sure she knows it's gonna be ok. Fuck, I really love this man. Yep, I totally just said that and inside my head, I hope. Tanya's eyes find mine as Grayson pulls her back placing a small kiss on her forehead.

"Right, Ma where is this brother of mine and how bad is it?" he asks calm, cool and collected. Me, on the other hand, I'm shaking from either the shock or the cool air warming up from the hospital and its overheated temperature. Grayson's hands reach out and seek out mine like it has a homing device attached to it for my body. Pulling me into him we take one step at a time as Tanya fills us in on the fact that it's a shoulder wound, he is lucky it barely missed the vital parts. He also has a woman with him and both are staying rather tight-lipped on who she is, what she's doing with him and where she is from.

"Believe me, I have asked all the questions, stomped my feet and rolled my eyes. I have even slammed my hands on my hips and put on my serious mum voice and they ain't budging," she says with a slight smirk but also with a slight annoyance. I stifle a laugh at her as Grayson shakes his head.

"Well Ma, do you really think now is the time for the Spanish Inquisition?" he shakes his head pulling me tighter into him as we enter through the glass doors that make that sucking whoosh sound as they open on their own after you push the green button. Lord, this place, it screams sickness and bugs and death. Tanya shakes her head at her son and his comment.

"Well, no, and now you just sound like your father, so stop talking." This family is just too much even in the midst of a shit storm and a shot brother they are still just so real. As we round the corner heading to the room that Tanner is in the curtain is flung open and nurses and doctors come spilling out. Tanner laying back his shot arm dangling from the bed and blood everywhere and I mean everywhere.

"What the fuck?" Grayson growls out as he hurries after the bed and has his brother and the young, and I do mean young girl in question mere moments ago falls from the room in tears. Tanners pale and pasty face is all I see in my eyes as I shut them. His eyes are a blank no-one home stare and Tanya starts screaming for answers as I try to wrap my arms around her body. A doctor comes toward us "I, um, well I tried to pull the bullet from his shoulder but accidentally nicked an artery on the way out. We are racing him into surgery to repair the damage and also the tissue and muscle that was shattered from the impact. The bullet didn't go all the way through his shoulder and the collarbone has taken full impact. I need to open it up so I can see what I am dealing with and just how bad it is.

"You ain't touching my fucking son. I want a real fucking doctor not someone in nappies," Derrek growls out and for the first time, fear slides down my spine, not for me but for the stupid doctor. Without missing a beat, the doctor keeps speaking and he may as well have signed his own death warrant as Derrek steps up into his space, fists clenched at his sides. "I will update you when I can, a nurse will collect you and take you all to a room to wait," he finishes taking off like a bat out of hell after the bed carrying Tanner. Grayson stands at the double doors watching as they push him through and all that is left behind are this mystery girls small sobs, Tanya's breathing, and a fuming Derrek who looks like he wants to chase the doctor down and beat the living hell out of him. My heartbeat echoes in my ears looking at the trail of hot red blood on the pearly over-shined hospital floor. Grayson turns on his heel, his hands running through his hair lifting his shirt slightly exposing his V above the waistband of his jeans. I have to squish down the moan that wants to slip free at the visual. Oh god, why am I turned on and thinking about this at this damn point in time? My cheeks redden and I feel like a fool, hoping no-one can read my features I turn my face into Tanya's shoulder taking deep breaths to calm my ass down. But Grayson who is so in tune to my body already notices straight away and pulls me into him. I look up into his handsome face as fire burns bright and hot in the depths of his captivating eyes. My gut twists knowing he knows what I am thinking about. He sends me a wink, kisses my forehead and rests there for a few moments. The small sobs from the girl push through our moment, kissing my forehead one more time he breathes into my hair that he wants answers and I nod into his warm chest. Tanya's arms wrap around me from behind and I turn into her hold as he strides over to the small frame of the broken girl on the floor lacing his hands under her armpits and picking her up. She slowly pulls her stare to meet his and

I watch her take in a deep breath as Grayson's voice breaks all of our thoughts. "Well love, best you start talking and fast," he says. I watch as fear flushes over her face and I'm worried she won't tell us anything if Grayson scares her, moving out of Tanya's warm embrace I step closer to them and send her a small smile of reassurance.

"Start with ya name, age, then move onto where, why, how, what and who." His voice leaves no room for thinking or arguments.

I instantly feel sorry for her and as I go to open my mouth to tell him to back off a bit her little deer in headlights look fades slightly as she opens her mouth and the quietest smallest voice dances out on a mere whisper. " Bethany, 20, Ringmaster, bar carpark and I have no clue why," her voice breaks "He's going to be ok right?" she questions as tears fall from her eyes dripping down her cheeks and falling onto her top that is covered in angry red streaks of Tanner's blood. Well, I hope its Tanners. Before I even think my mouth opens and words pour out "Doll you're not bleeding, are you?" I ask lifting up her arms and her shirt and inspecting her turning her in my arms and searching all over, "No, No its all um it's all."

"Tanners, my brother's blood." Grayson breaks as a nurse comes up to us. "Tanners family?" she asks looking around at all of us and we all in unison say "YES."

"Well, follow me to the room you can wait in," and like that we all just follow her like sheep following a shepherd. "Coffee, tea, juice, and fruit is all over here in the small kitchen and the bathroom is just through the door here. A doctor shall be with you as soon as they can," she says turning on her heel and just leaving us standing there in a room with air so thick you could cut it with a knife.

"Our boy needs to be okay," Tanya whispers into Derrek's chest as he wraps his arms tight around her.

"He will be," he clips so much certainty wraps around every word I feel myself relax a little as Grayson wraps his arms around me.

***

Seconds, minutes turned into hours and I'm not quite sure how many have passed but I feel the tension radiating through me like a livewire. Or that could be coming from Grayson when he keeps squeezing me tighter to his side like he is reminding himself I am still here. Blowing out a hard breath I try to relax into his side hoping to god Tanner gets out of surgery soon. I have only just met this family but in the short span of knowing them, my heart feels heavy thinking he won't be okay. I look around the small waiting room at all his brothers and his parent's somber faces and my eyes catch the woman that was with Tanner when he got shot. She hasn't said much and if I'm being honest with myself, she seems scared to death.

"He's going to be okay," I whisper so only Grayson hears me and he squeezes my hip in response. Shivers race through me as he absently rubs his thumb across my belly and I can't help the images that flash through my mind from the night before being tied to his bed as he worshipped every inch of my body. Casting my eyes down my heart beats in my throat at the thought of the marks being left behind from the rope. Blowing out a whispered breath when I notice there isn't any and I can't stop the little bit of disappointment as it flows through me that there isn't a reminder. Jesus, what is wrong with me? I wonder at the silly feeling. Grayson's heated breath slides down my neck as he bends to whisper in my ear sending a live current straight to my lower belly making me squeeze my legs together as the vibration of his voice assaults every one of my senses.

"Are you okay babe?"

"Shit," I curse trying to stop the small whimper bubbling up my throat. Turning my head, I nuzzle my face to the side of his neck trying to calm the raging need zapping through me, taking in a deep breath I regret it the moment I do as his intoxicating scent rushes through me. Right now at this moment, I don't care that we are in a hospital waiting room surrounded by his family. All I care about is having his rough hands sliding over my every curve as he pushes deep inside me.

"Walk with me," he breathes out and all I can do is nod as he pulls me to my feet and guides me out of the room. Sliding his arm around my waist we make our way down the pristine white corridor. Shit, I have had a taste of him and now I can't get enough of him. My panties are wet just over the mere thought of his body on mine. Looking up into his eyes I see so much worry washing through them that I make my mind up then and there to use the newfound sass and awakened sex devil inside me to take his mind off the stress of his brother even for just a few moments. *He needs it just as much as I do,* I tell my sex crazed head. Leaning into him I tug on his shirt so he bends down so I can whisper in his ear. "See that room over there," nodding my head in the direction of the semi-dark room. "You and me, 5 minutes to take your mind off all this."

Leaning back a little waiting for him to get the hint I chew on my bottom lip worried he might get pissed but that quickly washes away as a sexy curl kisses his lips. Stepping out of his arms I hurry my steps. Looking back at him over my shoulder, winking he gapes at me taken fully by surprise from my forwardness and probably realizing I'm actually serious. A low growl rumbles up his chest echoing around the walls of the sterile corridor sending delicious chills racing up and down my body. My cheeks pinken as I sneak a peek around his big body looking through the open door of the waiting room. My eyes look towards his mother and I'm sure his mother can read minds as her face pulls at the sides with shock mixed with humor as a smile cracks over her tired and strained features. Grayson blocks my view and clears the distance between us in an instant his hand cupping mine slowly and quietly we slip through the door into the empty room shutting the door behind him with a soft click that seems to echo around the small space. I don't even wait for him to make the first move or even say anything. I pull his hard body into mine my lips seeking his crushing together in a soul-consuming, lips, tongue, teeth kiss wanting it all. My body hums hungry for him, needy and hot. My skin prickles with heat from his touch alone as his hand slides down my back leaving a trail of fire in its wake. My hands seek the sides of his shirt and I pull it up and over his head fast a small chuckle leaves him dancing across my lips after I break the kiss to get it off, my eyes seeking his. "Funny, something funny? You have me aching at the most inappropriate time," I push out trying to rein in my breathing. "Nope babe just this and you," my mind flicks to what that means. "Huh?" I ask not having time to really think as all I want to do is get him naked and devour him.

"Nothing babe just this," he waves a hand between us a softness coats his face that has my heart melting, "I love you," he cups the side on my face in his big palm, rubbing his thumb across my cheek. Butterflies erupt inside my core as my knees go weak at the heaviness of his words, love, he loves me?! He said it before but this time it really sinks in. Sweet lord, I really do love him it wasn't a heat of the moment between us earlier, this feeling is all-consuming. With all that is going on it reminds me that life is short so when you love someone you love hard no matter the short time of knowing each other. Pushing my hands against his bare chest I push his massive body back towards the small single bed. The backs of his legs hit the cool steel bed frame, his deep chuckle bounces off the walls before turning into moans as I lean down licking, sucking his nipple into my mouth, his hand twists in my hair, breathing heavy. Sliding my hands down his hard muscles my fingers find the button of his jeans, fumbling fingers eager to get it undone. I sigh as I finally get it undone. Sliding the zipper down the whole time my eyes never left his as my lips slide from one hard nipple to the other. The primal hunger flaming inside those deep orbs has me squeezing my legs together as wetness coats my panties. Gripping my hair in both fists he yanks my mouth from his chest and slams his mouth down on mine, taking control from the first slide of his tongue as my hand wraps tight around his hard cock. Swiping the top with my thumb smearing the pre-cum as I go, growling into my mouth at the motion my body vibrates. I could coil undone right there at his feet. Ripping his mouth from mine breathing heavy his words come out hard, a command that has my body submitting.

"Naked now and bend over the bed."

Releasing him I make quick work of my clothes, reaching for my panties he doesn't give me a chance to take them off as he reaches forward and rips them straight from my body. The stinging sensation from the elastic only adds fuel to the fire that's lighting up my insides, before I can stop it a moan slips free. My palms hit the cool sheets on the bed, bowing my head taking in deep breaths I try to control the need to say fuck it and throw myself at him. But before I can catch my next breath one strong hand wraps in my hair, twisting so it's wrapped around his wrist he jerks my head back and my body curves like a cat pulling another moan from deep within.

"Princess, I'm gonna ride you so hard and deep you're gonna wanna scream my name, but your screams and whimpers are mine so bite your lip cause if any fucker walks in here seeing you lost in euphoric bliss, I'm gonna beat the shit out of them," he grunts in my ear. Darkness coats his words and all I can do is nod against his hold. Gripping the sheets in front of me my nails dig in, I bite down hard on my lip, a gasp leaves my throat as he slams into me hard and fast.

"Fuck," I grit pushing into him for more.

"Not a sound," his free hand comes down on my ass not once but three times. I have to close my eyes against the exquisite torture as he starts up a punishing rhythm, pressure mounts fast and hard, my legs shake, sweat coats my skin and I'm struggling to hold back the scream that wants to escape.

"So fucking tight," he whisper moans making me grunt as he hits deeper. Leaning over my back his husky voice pours through my ear.

"Suck it all up baby, pull the cum from my cock till you're struggling to hold it all in," his hot breath ghosts down my neck before he nips my ear and I hiss against the extra sensation. "Every time you move around I wanna know my cum is inside you making that baby." That does it, my world explodes, vision blurs and my pussy walls contract around his hard cock as if following his order and pulling the cum from him.

"Fuck," he grunts biting into my shoulder sending small shimmers of shocks running through me that have me gasping for breath.

"Sexy as fuck babe, knowing my cum will be dripping down your thighs as you sit with my family."

"Shit," I gasp my mind slowly catching up to his words as his husky chuckle runs through me.

"Asshole," I mumble only making him laugh louder and I can't stop the smile curling my lips and the thought of his cum smeared across my thighs around his family has my body heating all over again.

***

Laying in a tangle of arms, legs, and crisp white hospital linen we try to catch our breaths. My skin hot, flushed and dancing in the afterglow of pure fucking bliss. I could never grow tired of sex with him and I feel that I could never really get enough of his hands and the way they run over my bare skin making goosebumps ripple after each touch. "Princess, we'd better get dressed and head out as much as I want to lay like this with you forever we don't want my mum storming in here if Tanner comes out before us." His breath heavily laced in the sweet undertone of sex has my body shivering in his hold and all I can do is nod, not trusting my body to really move or even my voice to be normal and calm. Chuckling at my lack of movement he kisses my forehead relaxing me even more. "You were made for me." Nodding again as I shift my legs a little willing my body to move and I moan at the feel of his cum coating the insides of my thighs. Snaking his hand down my body he circles my clit pulling a moan from me as his fingers slip inside me, pushing in deep till my body tenses and begins to bow off the bed. "Fuck you feel good," leaning over me he kisses me hard before pulling back raising the fingers that were inside my pussy to his mouth and sucking them clean. I whimper at the loss as I felt my body ready to explode again but it's quickly replaced by a small moan at the sight of him licking our combined cum off his fingers.

"Fuck we need to get out of here before I take you again," with that he kisses me again and I grip his hair in my fingers pulling him into me, sucking our combined flavor off his tongue. My heart picks up speed as he squeezes my ass and pulls me into his body, automatically I start to move against his hard cock. Pulling back we're both panting heavily as we stare into each other's eyes.

"Yep, gotta get you out of this room," he grunts running a hand through his hair making me laugh.

"I have created a little sex kitten," he mumbles moving to get up and pulling the sheet with him as he goes.

"Is that a problem?" I laugh at the hungry look he shoots me.

"Up princess," he mouths to me folding the sheet into a messy ball and tossing it at me swiping it away. I pull my shaking body to the seated position as Grayson leans down picking up his jeans and boxers, and pulling his body into them. I watch in awe as each one of his muscles move freely over his tattooed body. "Fuck you're beautiful," I stutter out my voice as shaky as the pulse between my thighs. "Me?" he points to his now t-shirt covered chest looking around. "Nah Princess, you're the only beautiful thing in here." He breathes into me as his lips find my forehead placing a tiny fleeting but heavy kiss there. I pull my body into my clothes and pull my hair back into a not so sleek ponytail.

Walking over to the door he winks before bending and grabbing my ripped panties off the floor he brings them up to his nose and inhales deeply before stuffing them into his pocket with a grunt. "Damn," I murmur as he opens the door for me just as I'm about to step out Grayson is right behind me and his hands rest on my ass before sliding them around to rest on my belly his thumbs running small circles over my shirt covered belly. Sighing at the sweet touch I'm about to take a step into the corridor when a bed comes around the corner with a very groggy but a very much alive Tanner. He takes in my flushed just fucked cheeks and his face splits into a wide grin as he brings his good hand out to his brother making the orderly stop in his movements as he slurs out. "Well, nice to know you were worried about me brother," a laugh leaves him and Grayson follows with his own as his body relaxes more around me.

"Listen you little fucker, I knew you would be fine you just like to freak mum out and get all the fucken attention." Grayson laughs again when Tanner's smile takes over his whole face. Something flashes through his eyes followed sharply by sucking in air through his teeth in pain from the movement of the laugh. His eyes look around again as if he is looking for something or in this case looking for someone. Panic washes through his eyes when he doesn't find what he was looking for.

Reaching out I rest my hand against Tanner's good shoulder, Grayson growls in my ear when I touch his brother but I ignore his caveman ass, "She is ok, she's with your mum." I say softly to him, relaxing under my touch I pull my hand back when he nods and closes his eyes for a beat. The orderly begins moving him back down the corridor again and I catch his warm smile as he sends me a wink. Grayson wraps his arms around my waist and stops me from following. Pulling me back into his hard chest his voice deep in my ear when he speaks and if I was wearing any panties they would have melted off as his words burned through me all over again.

"My cum is inside you, possibly my baby growing in your sexy as fuck belly. You are mine so quit touching other men." Nodding my head, his jealousy runs hot and fast through me that I have to close my eyes against the new pulse radiating through me. I take a few deep breaths to calm my ass down so I don't push him back in that room again and let him show me again who I belong to. After a moment when I think I have my sex crazed body under control, I open my eyes and hum as his lips brush against my neck.

"Your brother is hurt and needs comforting right now, Player." I sass my smartass reply and it seems to create a thick sexual blanket around us. Before he can toss me over his shoulder and start beating his chest I push out of his arms making quick steps down the corridor laughing when I hear his heavy boots following fast on my heels as his voice rumbles out.

"Princess!" making me laugh harder and my body hum knowing I'm gonna pay for that later and I can't fucking wait.

Epilogue

Grayson

9 months later...

'Beautiful Crazy by Luke Combs' flows through the hallway as I open the front door of my house, a smile curls my lips as flashes of dancing with my wife on our wedding night slam into me. Putting my bag down on the floor next to the entry table, I place my keys on top wanting to check on my wife. She wasn't feeling good today, morning sickness has totally kicked her ass her whole pregnancy and today I told her I had enough of her pushing herself to get up every day to come to work. So I demanded she stay in bed and try to relax. She was pissed and then the tears came and it was nearly enough to break me but I knew it was better for her to be in bed at home and not in a cramped office with me hovering over her all day. Well, I don't think I hover, those are her words, not mine.

"Grayson," she calls out snapping me out of my thoughts as her husky voice slides over me in a smooth caress.

"Hey Princess, how was your d--" she cuts me off before I can finish.

"Get your ass in here now," her voice bordering on hysteria and has the blood pumping through my veins as I race into the living room. I stop dead in my tracks as Mackenzie is bent over at the waist gripping the back of the lounge, breathing hard. My cock twitches at the sight and I can't stop the growl escaping my mouth.

"Stop checking me out and get your ass over here," she pants. "FUCK," her fingers turn white from the death grip she has on the cushion, as her body bends a little more.

"You did this to me so fucking fix it," she hisses out whimpering

Shit, snapping out of my lust filled head I always seem to fall into whenever I am in the same room as my wife I snap into action and clear the space between us in seconds. Rubbing her back she hisses out making me pause in my movements.

"Just breathe baby," I murmur.

"What the fuck do you think I'm trying to do, have a fucking picnic?! I am fucking breathing you big brute, but it's not working," she gasps as tears swim down her face and I have to bite off a chuckle. When she gets worked up and pissed off the funniest shit flies out of her mouth. I have learned to just shut my mouth otherwise I just piss her off more.

"I cannot believe I let you do this to me," she whimpers as her body begins to relax a little. I ignore her comment because she fucking begs for my cock every fucking chance she gets and she knows it. Rubbing her back I watch as her grip lessons on the cushion wanting to get her ass to the hospital.

"What, now you are a fucking mute?" she hisses as her body comes up standing, still rubbing her back I place my hand on her belly and feel how tight it is bending slightly till my mouth is near her ear and hold back a chuckle when her body instinctively shivers at my nearness.

"Princess, if I say anything it will probably only piss you off further, so how bout we get your little ass in the truck and then get your ass to the hospital so we can have our baby," pulling back I smirk when I see her eyes closed. Her eyes snap open a flash with burning fire and somehow, I know it before she speaks that I fucked up.

"We?" she hisses leaning forward as another pain envelopes her. "Screw this we shit Player, I'm the one that's gonna be pushing..." panting she whimpers again. "I'm pushing this baby out, not YOU!" she grits out finally. She lets out a scream that rocks me to my core and I need to get her moving now. Without another word, I sweep her up into my arms, her head falls to my shoulder as she curls in on herself. Without giving a fuck about the music blaring through the speakers I march us out to the truck. Balancing her in one arm I open her door and as gently as I possibly can I slide her into her seat before pulling the belt around her belly and snapping it into place. As I go to lean back and shut her door, she grips my shirt, her words coming out hard and fast as she tries to catch her breath.

"You are never touching me again."

The possessiveness when it comes to my wife pushes forward at her words and I grit my teeth with the need to spank her ass and prove her words wrong. Taking in a deep breath I let it slowly out before I speak.

"You wanna be pissed and scream you go for it babe, but you are mine, this body is mine." Cupping the side of her face I run my thumb under her eye, catching a lone tear before it can fall.

"I'm sorry," she mumbles before I can say anything else.

"Don't be sorry my Princess." I kiss her lips softly and she sighs into my mouth just like the first time I ever kissed her and I feel her body melt for me.

"Let's go have a baby," I murmur above her lips. "Remember no girls only boys we have to think positive through this whole thing," I remind her knowing if she gave me a girl, I would probably end up locked up in a fucking jail cell if she came out looking anything like my wife. Her eyes shine and her giggle slips free seeming lost in thought and the pain is forgotten for a moment and if this is the way I can help and make it less painful then that's what I will do. I will talk her ear off just to hear her laugh and watch as that breathtaking smile overtakes her face. Letting me go I kiss her one last time before pulling back and shutting her door, racing around the other side of the car I jump in and start the motor.

"You know, oh wise husband of mine," she groans as she leans forward and braces her palms against the dashboard. "We don't get to pick and choose the sex."

"The night I got you pregnant babe I made a deal with God that I was only to have sons," I grit out feeling a cool sweat take over my skin at the thought of a little girl.

"We will see," is the last thing she gets out as the pain skyrockets through her and our world for the next four hours turns upside down and turned around as tears, screams and a lot of heavy breathing were involved. That shit was nothing like our wedding night but by the time the last push was done our son, Lucus King, was screaming into the world and for the second time in the last nine months my world was rocked, shifted and finally complete.

"I love you Princess," I murmur into her ear as she lays back against my chest feeding our son. My heart skips a beat as his cool blue eyes lock with mine and I know I would lay down my world for what is in my arms right now. Reaching over to the bedside table I grab my phone, searching for my music app I hit the song I found the other day and I hit play. As 'Die a Happy Man by Thomas Rhett' flows through the otherwise quiet hospital room I hold my family tighter as I sing to my wife.

"I love you, Player," her watery words float over the music ingraining in my soul and I know I made the right decision claiming her as mine over nine months ago.

Mackenzie is the beginning and end of my world and I wouldn't have it any other way.

The End
One Brother down & Three to go....

About The Author

Hi my name is Kay Maree and I'm a wife, mother of 3 and I love to write Instant Love with twists and turns with a bit of suspense thrown in.

My debut novel is called Angel Mine and was released in early 2017.

I live in Newcastle, on the New South Wales coast of Australia with my husband and three beautiful children. Between being a taxi for my children, and working full-time, I somehow find the time to write. It's something I love with a passion and with the encouragement of my very supportive husband, I have accomplished one of my dreams - releasing my first novel.

I hope you fall in love with my characters as much as I have.

I love reading and getting lost in a good book when I manage to snatch five minutes to myself.

Author Links
Available exclusively at Amazon

Angel Mine (Mine #1) ~ Dominic & Brooklyn
Kitten Mine (Mine #2) ~ Antonio & Katherine
Sugar Mine (Mine #3) ~ Sergio & Kirsty
Petal Mine (Mine #3.5) ~ Nico & Josie
Trixie Mine (Mine #4) ~ Theo & Trinity (Coming Soon 2018)

Other books by Kay Maree

Inked Temptation – Book 1 Inked Series
Shadow Game
Majestic (Midnight Crest Book 1)
Cherry Christmas ~ A Stone Brothers Trilogy

Follow Links

Facebook - @KayMareeAuthor
Twitter - MisKay85
Insta - miskay
https://www.facebook.com/groups/AngelsKittensSugars/

https://kaymareesmutlover.wixsite.com/contemporary-romance